ECHOES OF THE YOUTH.

SPRING HEELED JACK MEDIA

ECHOES OF THE YOUTH

Cover Art by: Luc D'Arceaux

First Edition
ISBN: 979-8-9888322-6-3

For catalog email or visit:
springheeledjackmedia@gmail.com
springheeledjackmedia.com

Echoes of the Youth.

a WISH Academy Anthology

DEDICATION

This anthology is dedicated to the families and loved ones who encouraged us to explore our voices and share our stories.

A special thank you to Aryn Youngless, whose vision, generosity, and unwavering support brought this collection to life. Your dedication to helping English students pursue their creative writing dreams has made all the difference — thank you for believing in the power of words.

INTRODUCTION

Welcome to this special collection of stories, crafted with imagination, heart, and determination by a remarkable group of student writers who have had the courage to share their ideas with others. Each piece in this anthology is a testament to the creativity, voice, and unique perspective that young writers bring to the world of storytelling. To the students: Your work matters. You've taken the leap to write bravely and authentically, and now your voices will ripple beyond the classroom—reaching new readers and inspiring fellow writers. Your creativity, hard work, and resilience are truly astounding. Thank you for joining us in this celebration of student creativity. We hope you enjoy every page

TABLE OF CONTENTS

TABLE OF CONTENTS

Sammie Buchner

Sammie Buchner is a student at WISH Academy High School who enjoys realistic fiction stories. She began writing after taking Ms. Avalos' English class for an assignment. When not writing, Sammie likes to film Youtube videos, ride horses, go shopping, go to concerts, and swim. This is her first published story.

Dream Vacation
by Samantha Buchner

I did it! Whoo-hoo! I won a 2-week trip to Paris due to winning an art competition last month. The entry form I had filled out previously said I could choose any place in the world and I chose Paris because me and my sister always wanted to go. The entry form also said that I could invite five people.

So, I grab my notebook, Flip to a blank page, and write down the five people I want to bring. I write down, "Taylor Swift, Mia (my sister), Jetta, Teddy, Annie aka (Annie The Nanny), Des. And Bri." Then I grab my phone and start texting people. First, I text Des, "I'm inviting you on a 2-week trip to Paris, and we leave tomorrow." I copied and pasted that text message to Annie and Bri. I figured I just tell Mia about Paris when she gets home from school, and I'll meet Taylor Swift in Paris because she's performing the Eras tour in Paris right now. I haven't gone to school today because I had a doctor's appointment.

Then I hear Mia come in through the door. I shout from my room, "Mia, Come in my room. I need to tell you something." Then Mia comes into my room. I tell her the big news, "Mia, can you come to Paris With me tomorrow?" "We leave at 11:00 a.m. tomorrow." Mia replied, "Yes, but I haven't packed yet." then my mom peeked her head into my room and said, "You should probably go to bed soon. You have an early flight." I just ate a quick dinner and then started getting ready for bed. Then I hopped into my bed and quickly fell into a deep slumber.

And then, before I knew it, it was the next morning, and my mom was yelling, "Sammie, get up. Annie's going to be here soon!" I quickly got up and sat at the end of my bed Then my mom came into my room and helped me get into my wheelchair. I hear Annie coming through the door, And then I shout, "Can you come into my room? I need help packing." As soon as my bag was packed, I zoomed into the living room to eat a quick breakfast. I had a Double chocolate muffin. Then me and Annie started going to the car. We are taking a van because we couldn't find a wheelchair accessible. Uber.

We scrambled to the airport and through security, and then, before I knew it, we were on the airplane, and then we were off to Paris. In my opinion, time goes by so fast on an airplane because you're just flying on doing anything except flying. So, before I knew it, it was nighttime, and the moon was smiling at me as we flew over the ocean. The time went by so fast because we were in Paris just like that. I was so excited my brain was exploding with adrenaline. And then, we went to baggage claim, got an Uber, our hotel and all that other boring trip stuff. The first thing we did was go see the Eiffel Tower. It was even taller in person. After we got back to our hotel, I was so surprised to see that it was already time for bed because Paris has a nine-hour time difference. And then, from that moment, our trip was jampacked with activity after activity.

Before I knew it, it was already time to go home. I sadly packed my things, and Annie helped me. And then we went down in the lobby and checked out. In my opinion, the checking out is the saddest thing on a trip. We so solemnly got back into a wheelchair-accessible rental van. And went back to the Paris airport as I waved bye-bye.

Z. Cruz

Z Cruz is a student at WISH Academy High School who enjoys fictional stories. Z began writing because he was inspired by inspirations. When not writing, Z likes to game and eat mac and cheese, along with reading very interesting graphic books. This is his first published story.

Untold Warnings
by Z Cruz

"I made a wish to understand all languages. But when I look at
the sky, all I see is dire warnings."

   I panic as I rush to the observatory on the hill. It felt as if hours
went by as I combed through the traffic in a hurry. Angry honks
and slurs were thrown in my direction, but I couldn't care less. I
needed answers, and I needed them now. I got to my
observatory, and not to my surprise, nobody was there. "Good," I
whispered to myself as I bolted towards the main part of my lab.
I don't remember a time where I've ever ran this fast in my life.
The door swung open, crashing into the concrete wall behind it.
I grabbed a notebook and immediately started writing down the
words. By this time, the sun had already started to rise, so the
warnings were disappearing. I was able to make out a few of
them, though. "Don't look them in the eye." "They are coming".
These don't make sense to me at all. *Who's they? Why are they
coming here of all places?* Everything is jumbled and confusing. I
turned to leave my lab, but I saw the mess I made while rushing
about. Spilled coffee on the floor, the door has several hinges off,
there is a table flipped onto its back, papers flung so high they
were just coming into sight. I stood there, unable to move for
whatever reason. My mind was lost in convoluted thought. I
quickly cleaned up my mess and headed home. My house is only
a 30-minute drive, but it felt like time itself was stuck in place,
my mind racing in a hundred different directions at a million
miles per hour.

What should I do in this situation, if anything at all? *Do I tell someone? Who should I tell?* Can I trust someone enough to tell them? Everything is so convoluted, and it's infuriating how there could be such a dire situation at hand, and I might be the only one who knows about it. Even if I did tell someone, what would they say? Would anyone believe me, or would I be labeled a maniac yelling nonsensical things to people? Everything about today feels like the world's heaviest weight fell on my shoulders, and I just want some sleep.

I woke up in a panic the next day, my body sore and sheets drenched with sweat. I turned to the clock next to me. It read: 11:32 pm. I breathe a sigh of relief as I plop back into my puddle. After cleaning that whole mess up, I made myself some breakfast. Plus, I can just feel my bones getting stronger. As I grab a towel to take a shower, I see something in the corner of my eye. Something moving. I almost snapped my neck, looking in that direction. It was in my office. I slowly creep towards the glass door. The floorboards creak with each step. I slowly open the door to see nothing there. Everything was in the exact same place. Everything except for all the writing on the walls. I had no recollection of writing anything in my office, let alone even entering the room. I studied all the symbols and pictures carefully. Noting down and taking pictures of everything. I was just about to draw the last little diagram of what looked like to be some kind of manlike figure before they started jumbling again. This time, into words I could actually understand. I don't know if it was my brain or they were physically making the words appear in a language that may or may not have been different from their own, but I knew I could understand it. I immediately started taking a video of all of it.

Everything was moving around at a lightning-fast pace, it was as if the letters themselves were alive and trying to send a message… and quickly too. I jotted down as much as I could but some of the words were jumbled and incomprehensible. All I could make out was a bunch of numbers in the order of: 103072128927. Soon after I had jotted down the numbers, I had been hit in the head from behind.

  I had woken up, or so I thought. When I opened my eyes, I didn't see my bedroom ceiling like I had hoped, or my office ceiling. Actually, I didn't see any ceiling at all. I was just standing, or better yet floating, in what was like a dark abyss. I couldn't tell what was what except for my hands. Everything in that moment felt so nauseating. It felt as if I was moving but not moving at the same time. Just as I felt as if I was gonna throw up, something gave me some sort of sense of direction. A bright blue, glowing light in the distance. The longer I stared at it, the more I realized it was coming straight at me and at a scarily fast pace, too. I started panicking. Flailing my arms around as if that would be of any use to me. I bet I looked like a chicken trying to fly. My entire life just flashing before my eyes. All the things I've experienced, everything that I said, that have changed my life. As the beam approached me, it slowed down until it came to a direct stop right above me. I closed my eyes and accepted my fate. No idea how much time has passed, honestly I think I took a nap because I felt as if I had drifted back from where I was before. I looked around me but there was nothing except empty darkness. Honestly it was kinda getting cold out here… wherever I was. As I just floated around in this void, I remember the light I saw before I knocked the hell out. *Honestly, it was probably the best sleep I've had in a while.*

And I saw what looked like a spaceship of some sort. As I stared at it, a small light started surrounding me. All of a sudden, I was blinded by a white light. Then, the whole world faded into darkness as I blacked out. *Huh…?* I thought sleepily. I didn't know what horrors I could be met with if I opened my eyes, so I felt my surroundings. *Soft… and wet?* No more dewy than wet. I tried to slowly open my eyes, but it felt as if they were glued shut. After trying for a bit, I tried to move my arms, but, to my surprise, I couldn't move them. My arms felt as if they were 200 pounds weights. So much time has passed to the point where I don't know how long it's been. It could've been a few seconds, hours, days. Maybe I'm just overthinking it, and nothing has happened at all. Honestly, how can you blame me for overthinking though? All this has happened, and I still don't know a single thing more than when this all began. The only sense of "time" I even had was the blinding light that was shining onto me. I don't even know if that's the actual sun or if it's just a super big and really bright flashlight that's slowly circling around me. I can't even tell if I'm thinking this or if I'm saying this out loud. Through what felt like hours of just me rambling on to myself about how much I hate how this happened to me and mentally driving myself insane, I tried my arms for maybe the 50th time, and I felt movement. I immediately tried to lift my arms towards my eyes and pried them both open. Almost immediately, I was blinded by the sight of that dumb fireball in the sky. The dewy feeling I felt on my neck and arms was some weird looking grass. It had the color of the inside of a blueberry. As I slowly picked myself up from the ground, I noticed the air smelled a bit smokey, as if someone was barbequing. I followed the trail of heaven for a while before I reached a small clearing on a hill of trees.

Through this, I saw a small town with a tower of billowing smoke coming out directly in the middle of it. It looked like there was a pit with a bright glowing light where the smoke was coming from. I decided I was gonna explore the town, but before I could even take a step, an arrow unlike any I've ever seen landed right in my foot. It took a bit for me to completely process what had just happened as I was still a bit woozy from the bright light from before. But as I came to a clear mind, the pain hit me so hard I felt as if I had taken several gunshots to that one area. I fell to the ground, rolling down the hill. Each turn was more painful than the other, so painful that it got to the point where I would almost black out with every pulse my heart did. *This is the SECOND TIME. I'm done with this mess. I just wish all this never happened*, I said in my head. Then, I heard a voice in my head that wasn't mine. Something darker, as if I felt its presence in my head. "*Say it again. Say it out loud.*" It said with a menacing voice. I screamed it so loud I don't remember even saying it. Then I blacked out. Again.

I woke up for what I hope is the last time in this seemingly endless loop of waking up and knocking out almost immediately. *This is getting tiring*, I said with a yawn. That yawn was abruptly stopped when I sat up and saw a gun pointed at my head. I notice I'm actually home now. My office across from the room I'm in is still a mess. I look towards the figure. It doesn't have any physically defining features except for arms, legs, a body, and a head. There's no face, no chest, no nothing. It was as if I was staring into an entity made of only void. I slowly put my hands up to hopefully show that I come in peace. The entity's gun, it doesn't look like any normal gun. It was like something from a video game. All high tech looking, probably shoots lasers, silver colored, cool looking grip.

The entity slowly put the gun down and slowly turned its head to the side. As if it was showing me it was confused by my actions. Then, the entity slowly reached its hand out, grabbed my face, and squeezed. And just like that, I felt the most intense wave of drowsiness I've ever felt before. *AGAIN??* I thought as my eyes grew heavier and heavier. I fought the best I could to stay awake in that moment. Felt as if time was moving as slowly as possible. My eyes felt as if they were made out of iron. I could feel myself giving in to the growing intensity of the sleepiness. Every method I tried, pinching, pain, scare, and every other kind of torture I could possibly get my hands on didn't work in the slightest.

Zar Zar

Zar Zar is a student at WISH Academy High School who enjoys exploring human emotions through the lens of real-world tragedies via fiction. He began writing after taking Ms. Avalos' English class where she inspired him to tell his own stories. When not writing, Zar Zar likes to sleep, eat, read, and play video games. This is his first published story.
XOXO

Four Bullets to the Chest
by Zar Zar

"He's dead," the officer says gruffly. I look down at Jonah, his head lying limp on my shoulder, his life flowing out of his body and into the alley like spilled crimson wine. The backdoor of the bar hung open, the cloying scent of alcohol and smoke filling my nose. The man I was supposed to marry the next day was dead in my arms, my formerly white shirt now matching with the blood pooling beneath us.

"How?" I ask. The officer looks at me and seems to be running through options in his head. "Four bullets to the chest."

"What?"

"I'm sorry for your loss, sir, but we need to ask you some questions."

"Why?"

He sighs and runs a hand over his pale face. He says something into his radio, but I'm not paying attention. A few moments later, I'm gently lifted to my feet and guided towards an ambulance. I sit on the edge of the bumper and am given a weighted blanket and a cup of water.

He's dead.

I don't register when the tears start falling. All I know is that one moment I was sitting in the ambulance, and the next, sobs racked my chest. I dropped the cup, and as it cracked on the pavement, I wrapped my arms around myself. A storm ripped through me, an endless flood of tears and wails.

He's dead.

I curl up into a ball and lay on my side in the ambulance, a puddle forming beneath my cheek pressed against the cold floor. I don't know how long I stayed there, screaming and crying as everything I've ever loved bled on the concrete. He was so still. So, so still. I hear the paramedics put my heart on a stretcher and move him to the ambulance next to mine. The scent of iron and his cologne hits my nose.

He's dead.

I heave and the dinner we shared less than an hour ago leaves my stomach, then the world goes black.

The sound of a quiet praise song is the first thing I hear. I lay there with my eyes closed and try to comprehend the lyrics, but I get nothing. Next, I hear someone gently crying next to me, as if afraid her sorrow would impede the music. I try to open my eyes but can't muster the energy, so I settle for turning my head towards the crying.

"Ma?" I mutter. My throat is dry. I wonder how long I've been out. I hear her shift and clear her throat.

"Hey, baby. How're you feeling?" she asks, as her voice breaks. The question hangs in the air for a long time, but no matter how hard I try, I can't answer. Finally, I manage to open my eyes. I'm in a hospital room, the walls painted a baby blue with white trim. She must've noticed me taking everything in, and said, "You passed out in the ambulance after…"

He's dead.

"Ma?" I whisper.

"Yes, baby?"

"Jonah. He's…gone?" For some reason, my voice tilts up into a question, though I meant to just state it. Maybe there's some part of me hoping that once he was brought into the ambulance, the bullets left his chest and all his blood flowed back into his body. That he'd walk through the door to my hospital room and joke about how he'd scared me so bad I fainted.

The look in my mothers' eyes told me that wouldn't happen.

"I'm so, so sorry, Elijah. They couldn't save him," she said. I shouldn't be surprised. I watched as the light drained from his eyes like the red from his chest. He died on my lap, holding my hand until he could no longer.

"Ma?" I say.

"Yes?"

"I don't think I'm okay." I've never felt this vulnerable before. Like each layer of my being was peeled away to expose a bleeding, reeling soul, torn in half. Ma turns up the volume on her phone a little bit, filling the room with the soft music. I realize that it's one of Jonah's favorites. She scoots onto the small bed and wraps her strong arms around me.

"We're not going to be okay for a long while, baby, but someday we will be. I don't know how or when. But we will be." she says. Even as my world is crumbling around me, I feel a little more solid in her embrace. I cry, but this time it's not the malevolent storm from the ambulance, but quiet. Quiet like when I heard Jonah stop breathing. Quiet like what the home we shared will sound like. Quiet like the wedding bells at church today. We cry for what could have, should have been, and for what reality decided it's going to be.

We stay like that for a long time.

Jerron Fowler-Presley

Jerron Fowler-Presley is a student at WISH Academy High School who enjoys the genre, writing fantasy and adventure stories, and exploring human emotions through fiction. He began writing, I started writing after taking Ms. Avalos' English class, where she inspired me to make my own narratives. When not writing, Jerron likes to bake and play volleyball. This is his first published story.

The Only Change is You
by Jerron Fowler-Presley

"Hey Chuck" Bernie whispered across the room.

"What" I groaned.

We had a sleepover the previous night. I was drowsy with the room filled with silence as I'm trying to collect my thoughts.

"What" I mutter.

"You wanna sneak out and go to the creek," said Bernie.

This motion was very idealistic. It felt as if he was joking. If he was it was as funny as an elderly person falling, not very amusing. My father had always been an overprotective person from as far back as I can remember. Any attempts to do anything outside of my father's criteria of safety or leaving out his care were promptly ended.

"You know my father isn't gonna go for that if we get caught."

"Chuck, you're Fourteen and you've never been to the creek at all," he says as he folds his blankets.

"This is probably one of the last chances you're gonna get Since you getting old, We start high school in a week and I don't want you to miss out on it and regret it."

I only caught half of what he said but most of what I heard hit me like a brick. It felt as if an impending crisis had been placed on my shoulders.

Bernie has always had my best interest in mind, that's just the type of person he was since as far as I could remember Chuck was my best friend. He had long brown hair with freckles and hazel eyes. He has always been the tallest boy in our grade at school and super friendly. he'd lived only across the street from me and heck our parents were friends. Well, that was until my mom had passed, One day my mom took me to the park when I was two years old. Apparently, we had just been playing at the playground when a man approached us with a knife, my mom tried to put up a fight by grabbing me and running. But she had been stabbed by the assailant while trying to flee. The only reason why this didn't continue further was because my mom had happened to be escaping down the same path as a cop and from there, the cop shot him dead. When my dad got the news he was apparently in shambles.

When my father had heard the eyewitness testimony he shut down completely only focusing on me. Nowadays my mom is a sensitive subject, And just when I bring up with my dad he seems to shoot down the conversation just as fast as it came up. The thought of missing out floods my mind to the point where I can't enjoy my sugary cereal. "Bernie, I made up my mind" With a serious look on my face.

"We're going to the creek," I announced.

The Creek had always been a staple of our rural community for the kids. It was filled with trees partnered with a big lake. It's always been a dream to go there. Every kid's weekend plans at my school have somehow always included the creek. I felt left out like an oddball, which didn't help since me and my father seemed to be the only brown people in Texas. My dad eventually stumbles out of his room and the smell of cigarettes fills the room. My dad had always been a heavy smoker but never smoked in front of me, only in his room or always out of view. When he does, the smoke smell lingers in my room. my dad greets Bernie. "Hello Bernie good morning." Bernie wave.

"Good morning sir." Bernie says my father walks over to me and kisses me on my forehead.

"Good morning, Dad."

"Good morning Chuck." He smiles brightly.

"What are your plans for the day? School is starting in a week are you ready for it?"

"Yes, Dad I'm ready for school." I ignore his first question.

My dad smiles in response and he starts his daily routine, without fail it always starts with him making a cup of coffee. It sometimes feels as if he needs it to function because he drinks it like it is medication. His second step in his routine is always to go into the bathroom. As soon as he enters the bathroom I realize this might be my last chance to leave outside of his view. I look at Bernie, he looks back at me, and I nod.

I go to grab my phone while Bernie heads to the door. After grabbing my phone I start to head towards the door I look back at the bathroom door take a deep breath and take a step out the front door.

I look outside and it is bright and warm out. We lived in a place where you never really heard loud cars from highways. I take a deep breath taking in the smell of flowers and cut grass. As soon as I do, like clockwork my father comes stomping and stammering out of the bathroom. "CHUCK GET BACK HERE!" he yells.

I turn over my shoulder to see my bald father screaming charging at me like a bull. I Start panicking not knowing what to do I freeze. My dad runs up to me while huffing and puffing he grabs me by my shirt collar. And starts berating me with questions and yelling at me, "WHERE WERE YOU GOING?"

"WHY WERE YOU TRYING TO LEAVE?"

"DON'T EVER ATTEMPT SOMETHING LIKE THIS AGAIN!" screams my dad. I turn to Bernie to see him a distance away, Staring. I look back to my father and breaking away from his grasp I exclaim.

"Why won't you let me live my own life? Why do you have to be so controlling? Huh. I just want to go to the creek And hang out with my friend. That's all I ever wanted." I paused looking to the ground as tears began rolling down my cheeks.

"I stepped outside of this yard for a second and you freaked out on me. I just want to fit in."

My face became hot from the crying. I began to look up and I watched my dad start to cry, this was the first time I had ever seen him cry. He began to sob uncontrollably, my emotion turned from frustration to confusion.

"I never meant to be controlling, I just- I just wanted you to be safe. I don't want to lose another person I care about because of a decision I made." he paused and took a deep breath. " Look son it's time you knew. When your mother died I was supposed to be with you guys but I decided to stay home since your mom wanted me to rest," he sighed a heavy breath like what he said lifted a weight off his chest

"I should've insisted on coming, put up more of a fight you know" at this point the tears began flowing again from both me and my dad.

"After your mom died I began to drink obsessively and became a drunk alone with a toddler. I had only realized you're my top priority after a bottle almost fell on you," he said "Look son I just want what's best for you. If you truly feel like you need to go then you can go. I'm so sorry son."

I lunged towards my dad to reach for a hug.

"I- I Never knew you went through all of that," he stammered.

They sat together hugging on the side of the road for five minutes until Chuck's dad urged him off to go to the creek. Nervously Chuck looks back at his dad and waves before he goes on walking with Bernie to the creek.

"What was that?" asked Bernie.

"Acceptance" replied Chuck.

"You sound dumb," Bernie laughed.

"Yeah, guess so," chuckled Bernie.

The End

Jason Valencia

Jason Valencia is a student at WISH Academy High School who enjoys writing fantasy and adventure stories. He began writing on December 17, 2024, "I started writing after taking Ms. Avalos' English class, where she inspired me to tell my own stories". When not writing, Jason likes to play soccer and video games. This is his first published story.

Hell-a
by Jason Valencia

September 6, 2020

It was a typical day at Rival High. Me and my friends were just relaxing on some benches near the baseball court, talking, messing around, when we noticed a pod flying towards us. It hit the fences, breaking them and landing not too far from where we were all at. We were curious at first, but then we heard noises coming from it, like some sort of being. We were told not to approach, but I didn't listen. I walked up close to see, but was pulled away by my classmates.

It was then we saw the being. It looked like something not from here—a big female-looking creature with a giant staff, no face, and looked as if it's a ballerina, with her legs being covered with what looked like a dress, but it seems like it was part of it. It sends out a big screech, running to a teacher, ripping her piece by piece like a butcher. It then eats her.

We all see in fear. We see she was not alone, as more pods arrive. It's her army. They wreak havoc across the school and city. We all ran out, got home safe. We all see the creatures fall back and go to their queen. They are all being controlled like a hive. We see from our windows the queen is making a tower to hide behind.

For the rest of the day, we wondered if they were to attack again. We got confirmation from the school principal that we still had school the next day.

At first, my parents were a bit skeptical about it but ended up agreeing that I had to go. So the next morning, I arrived to school still scared at what could happen if those things were to attack again.

Period one started, and this time it was different. We didn't do work at all. It was like we were just there to be there. A couple of hours go by and then we get news from the intercom. It was an unfamiliar voice saying:

"Attention Rival High, there is a big announcement we need to share. Report to the fields. That means everyone."

We all gathered our stuff and walked there. Me and my friends met up. We kept talking and speculating—what's this announcement? We got there. Our parents were there too. We were concerned.

"Is this about the invaders?" says my friend George. George is the smartest guy in the group. I've known him since 4th grade. The dude is so smart he made a prototype for a gun that shoots green rays that explode. We don't really know what to call it yet, but he says he wants to finish it and show the US so they would use it for the wars. It's his dream to be a scientist for the government, to help research more weapons to help combat the worst of foes.

"Maybe, but why the military?" says Violet, my cousin. She lost her parents crossing the border from Mexico. My parents took her in when I was 7. She's 2 years younger than me and was 2 grades down from me.

We found her right outside the border as we got the call to pick her up. After we did, we tried asking her what she saw and what happened to her parents. She explained that her parents were kidnapped by the cartel and she saw them get tortured and brutally killed right in front of her. From then on, she can't forget that image from her head. She swore one day she would take revenge on them. When my parents took her in, we were like siblings, so we don't call each other cousins—we call each other brother and sister.

"I guess they might use the school as a military base?" says Mark. He is the funny one in our group, but when you mess with him—well, let's just say you're going to sleep for quite a while, to say the least. He was the first person I met from the group, and boy, are we inseparable. We swore on each other no matter what —we won't let this family fall apart.

"Well, lucky for you, I might have the answer," says Stacy. She's Mark's twin. She's quite sneaky—like, very. She would often scare us just by sneaking up. She also snuck into the school office at night and found documents for secret plans the school might do at some point. One she found might just be about this. When she first found the documents, she never told the group until recently. She stole those docs a year before all this. Why hide it, you may ask? Well, it was because some of those docs would scare us all, but she didn't want us panicking. The only person she told was Reina. Who's Reina? Well, I'm glad you asked.

"Oh, the documents—I mean maybe, but it's a long shot," says Reina.

At first, when I met her back in 4th grade, she wasn't quite talkative. She had just come from Brazil during the civil war. She didn't quite know English at first, but then learned how to speak it. She knew Portuguese, and me coming from Mexico, I did not know it, but she kept one language in secret—it was Spanish. So one day, I walked up to her to see if she would talk, and she did, and that's how we became friends. When she learned about my cousin one time and her past, she could relate since they were running from bad places. The only difference with Stacy is that she didn't lose her parents, but they were abusive, so she was put into foster care, then adopted into a loving family. This was after meeting Mark, so she's the second person in the group.

"Hmph, we will see, girls. Just you wait."

And who said that, you might ask? Well, that was me—Daniels. I'm the founder of the group. I first made the group three years ago. I've come from Mexico, like I said. I left with my parents when I was 3. The road was long, but we missed the cartel. We left the country because my parents wanted a better life for me —just like my cousin.

We were in the fields for a while when finally the captain of the military came in. He spoke out: "Well, good evening everyone. I'm hereby to tell you something about these invaders and what's going to happen to the school and to all of you."

He continued: "First of all, the invaders—they are from space. We've been observing them for 20 years while they were in their pods. They are very hostile, and all they want is to eradicate our race. So I'm hereby giving you an option:

A. You stay here in Los Angeles but go through military training and become soldiers.

Or B. You go to Las Vegas with your parents and miss out on all the fun.

Now, why am I using a school as an army, you may ask? Well, it's because of the Russian war. All our troops were deployed in Warsaw as the war escalates."

The Russian war is a war that's been going on since 2014. It started because Russia was attacking NATO countries—they have plans of bringing back the USSR, but we've been combating ever since.

"So after today, those who will stay will stay home. Those who will leave will come to the school, and we will take you all to the secret bunkers in Las Vegas."

"The choice is yours. Return home and decide whether to stay or not."

We all went home. My dad says, "Stay. We know you can do this."

And so I stay. The only reason they let me stay is because I've known the basics of being a soldier since my dad was one. He taught me what I should know. So I stay. So does Violet—she also went through the same thing as me.

The next day, all the parents and all the schools of L.A. would join in at the same time, with them all being separate territories.

We were all sent home to relax until we go into training. All my friends now live with me and Violet in our house. And that night, we asked the same thing:

"Why use us and not more adults?"

Well, luckily someone had an answer:

"Because they wanted to test how middle schools would do as an army, as they think we learn faster."

So we got our answer. And now we are satisfied. So we all went to bed to prepare for training.

Two years later.
November 7, 2022

It was a cold night in the rain. Me and our group would start the mission.

"Strike team, this is your intel guide, here to guide you through the mission. Request backup if needed."

And so we proceeded, entering a factory run by Russians. We entered, saw two guards. Mark walked to one and snapped the guard's neck. I grabbed my knife and stabbed the other in the neck.

"Weapons ready?" says George.
"Ready," me and the rest claim.

"Alright, my mark—kill all that moves," says George.

"On 3—1... 2... 3!" says George, as we run through the next room.

One by one we shot down multiple Russians. They were everywhere—on top of stairs and on platforms. I shot down three until—

"I'll meet you guys up front," says Daniels. I yell out, "Brother, no!" as he left and ran through the doors. "Violet, don't let him do what he likes," says Reina.

As we approach the last room, we hear some gunfire from inside the room—but the enemies did not shoot at us. Slowly, the gunshots stop. We entered the room and saw Daniels grabbing the Russians' intel on their plans.

"There, problem solved," says my brother.

"You could have gotten yourself killed, you bastard," I say.

"What? We got what we wanted," says my brother.

"Yeah, but think twice before acting upon," I say.

"Yeah, whatever. Let's just go home," says my brother.

We got home and we had a great feast. Me and the girls cooked and the boys were all working on George's project—the prototype gun. As we cooked, I kept thinking: Why does my brother keep acting ahead?

We all ate like a family, enjoying the food as we looked at the intel we got from the Russians.

Now why are Russians here? Well, since they heard the creatures arrived, they had ideas of coming here to steal weapons and gather intel on us so they could strike in secret. Me and the group would be tasked with these missions since we were all the best at this. We call ourselves Hell-a's Finest—Hell-a being Los Angeles. We call it Hell-a because of the invaders. The Butchers, we call them—because the way they kill is very brutal, like they were some autopsy doctor or something like that.

We all gathered the info and sent it to the captain. In the intel, it said they had been developing a weapon in secret to take control of the Butcher army and the queen, but it's still in development.

We went to sleep. The next morning, we woke up, ate breakfast, grabbed our stuff, and arrived at school. When we arrived, we got the respect of everyone. This is because we are the best team on base, with my brother having the most attention. We all got to first class, and we all got called to the office. The captain told us:

"You did so well last night, but we still have more to do. I have a new mission for you all. Go to your computer to access it."

We went to the computer to see what they would give us, and the computer, one by one, called our names and said our roles:

"George, you are support. You will be given med packs for the team."

"Daniels, you are sniper support."

"Mark, Violet, Reina, Stacy, De$%@, and Sca#%!—you all are aggressive. Run in, clean house. Your objective is to eliminate all members of the building and secure the intel."

"Wait, who are those and why are they blocked out?" I say.
"Beats me, let's ask that officer," says Mark.

We walked up and were told that they are secret allies that will fight with us. We were all confused. We all thought it was just a mission for us. We didn't worry too much, so we went to lunch. And that's when a surprise came to us:

"Surprised to see us?"
It was Devon and Scarlet.

"Dev, Scar—you sons of...! Devon, why fake your death?" says my brother.

"Well, we had some things to run away from," says Devon.

"Well, it don't matter—we're glad to see you both," I say.

"Wait, who are they?" says Mark.

"Well, I'm glad you asked. They were me and my brother's friends. One day, we went sneaking into a factory to look for cartel members, but things went wrong. We thought that Devon had died in an explosion, and Scar had to be moved to the UK since her visa expired," I say.

"Well, it's good to have you. Welcome to the club," says George.

We all talked, made jokes, drank, and then got home to prepare.
We got to the location. It was a house we'd never seen.

"No matter—it would be easy," we all say.

We went in and got out. My brother was pissed because he was
sniper support, but we all did what we do best.

"Mark, Stacy, Scar—you take back. Violet, Devon, Reina—you're
with me," says George.

We all rushed in and killed what moved.
*Damn, why do I have to be sniper support? There's nothing I can shoot
at. Oh well, I have no choice... wait—maybe I could rush in on my own.
Yes.*

As I walk toward the house, I could hear my radio make noise.

"Delta 4, what are you doing? You're supposed to be supporting,"
the captain says. "I'm going in to support," I say. "Well, I hope
you know what you're doing," says the captain.

I run in, bashing through doors, shooting the enemies, and
caught up to the group.

"Daniels, what the hell are you doing here?" says George. "Sorry
guys, but I was being sniped at," I say.

everyone on the spot. I wanted that new rank so badly. I needed
to be so quick—but suddenly:

"Daniels! Get over here!" Mark yells out.

"What?" I say, not knowing what just happened.

"Why do you have to rush in and not listen to the order? My sister got shot in the leg because of you," Mark yells.

"If you keep doing this, more bad things will happen. Worse—someone could die."

"Yeah, well, you all had to be more faster," I say.

"Dude, we do things slow and easy—none of this fast speed-run type thing. Just think twice before rushing in," says George.

"You are responsible for her injury. More of this, and I will have to tell the captain," says Mark.

"Fine. I was just trying to help," I say.

We all got home, ate dinner, and went to sleep. The next morning, we rested. Me and the boys went hunting while the girls took care of Stacy's leg so she could get back up. We went hunting for hours. As we got home, we got a call from the command center at school:

"Listen up, you boys will be sent to kill Butchers on Monday. Be ready. High-level threats are in that area."

We got home and we all ate what we hunted—rabbits, fish, and cow. We were told not to tell the girls about that operation and keep it a secret, because Stacy might want to join in, but she's forbidden to do work until she's fully healed.

We got prepared and went straight to work. I woke up to the boys gone, so I made breakfast for the girls and we all ate. We saw that the van was gone.

"It is their guys' day, I guess," says Stacy.

We all didn't worry much, as we knew they could do good together. Hours go by—and they arrive.

"Daniels, you should have listened! How many times do we have to tell you?" yells Mark.

"So what? We did it good, didn't we?" says my brother.

"Yeah, but you keep rushing in. Why do you keep doing this? Stop, bro. This isn't a race," says George.

They were all pissed because my brother kept rushing in instead of sticking with the group.

"Guys, guys, calm down. It's over. You all did well," says Devon. "Fine," says Mark.

We all ate dinner and we went to sleep. After that day, my brother never listened. After so many operations, he kept doing the same thing—he kept rushing in and in. And because he was so impatient, we kept warning him, but he wouldn't listen.

Until one day.

We were going to raid a Russian base—which was a school—and the students were part of the Russian army.

We were told to make a strike team. It was our first raid. We were given a small army to combat the Russians. This was Operation Blue Star, where we would destroy the school and everyone there.

We all went back home to rest and prepare. As we were there, Devon had a game to play. He took us to his house and found his old Nintendo 64. We all decided to play Super Smash Bros for a while to relieve the stress and tension building up. After playing, Devon got up and said:

"Everyone, listen up. I'm here to tell you all how thankful I am to be part of this family and all the fun we have. Tomorrow will be a day to remember. May the gods bless us all."

We all yelled in support. We went to bed, and we all called our parents before sleeping.

"Hey kids, how are you all doing?" says Mom.

"We are doing great. We just got home from the meet-up at school. They gave us an army for this mission," says my brother.

"How's Steven, Dad?" I say. Steven is our brother. He was born a year before.

"He is doing just fine. Just crawling around, having fun, just relaxing," says Dad.

"That's nice," I say.

We all talked for minutes and then we said good night and went
to sleep.

Thursday, February 23, 2023.
*Damn, Daniels. Why won't he listen? We've been at this for almost a
year. I'm getting tired of this.*

We arrived at base, grabbed our weapons, and drove off. When
we arrived at the Russian school, we waited hours to strike, so we
slept in the meantime. We were supposed to strike at 8 p.m.

It was 8 p.m.—time to strike.

We went off and killed everything in our path—butcher
Russians, everything. It was going so well until Daniels does it
again.

"Daniels, what are you doing!!" I yell out.

"Don't worry—I got it!" he yelled back.

That's when the backstab happens.

"Well, you guys did your part. Now it's my turn," says Devon as
he proceeds to shoot my sister Stacy in the kneecaps. She
screams in agony as I rush toward her, but then I hear an
explosion. I watch as a group of our men are knocked back by
the blast. We all fall back. The mission was a failure.

When we got home, everyone saw Stacy injured. She couldn't
walk, so we dropped her off at the hospital.

The doctors said there was a chance she could heal, but the odds were 50/50. I yell at Daniels for what he did.

"We lost soldiers because of you. You got my sister injured all because you rushed in!"

"I'm sorry, bro," he says.

"Don't be sorry. No more of this. When Stacy is cured, I'm out. No more of this. I don't want to lose her," I reply. Daniels leaves, and I stay at the hospital.

Weeks later, I feel like a mess. I got her injured, and now my brother is leaving for Las Vegas with his parents. Damn, I should have known better.

"I know this is your fault, but learn from it and heal. You were just impatient," says Reina.

"But I messed up badly. Now Mark hates me," I say.

"You did, but it's okay. We all make mistakes," says Reina.

Her words give me some confidence. It helps a lot. I gather the team for a mission briefing.

"Okay, listen up. I know this fall is a lot to take in, but we have to fight on," I say.

"Yeah, but how? We don't have Mark or Stacy," says my sister.

"Yeah, but we have the gun," says George.

"The gun? Isn't it a prototype?" I ask.

"Who said anything about a prototype?" George replies.

We walk into the garage, and George begins explaining.

"Before the mission was set, I made sure to finish these guns. I created seven new weapons for everyone and gave them names. The Ray Gun, Daniels' weapon—this was the first one we made, and I finished it first. It shoots explosive projectiles, and now it's stable. I also made the Wunderwaffe DG-2, a gun that shoots lightning and vaporizes enemies. Then there's the Thunder Gun, a massive weapon that can knock back multiple enemies into oblivion. The Ray-K 84, much like the Ray Gun, but fully automatic. The Winter's Howl, a pistol that can freeze enemies. The Jet Gun, a weapon that sucks enemies in and shreds them to pieces. And last but not least, the DRI-11 Beam Smasher, a laser gun, basically."

"Alright, so who's in and who's out?" I ask. Everyone raises their hands.

"Then it's settled," I say, "and we all grabbed a weapon of our own. Violet grabbed the Thunder Gun, Reina took the Wunderwaffe, Scarlet got the Winter's Howl, George the DRI-11, and I grabbed the Ray Gun. We all piled into the van and headed to get Stacy and Mark. Stacy can walk now, so I asked—

"I'm sorry, but now we have firepower. Are you two in or out?" I yell.

Mark walks up and says, "Give me the gun. We're both in."

We handed them the guns, they geared up, and we went to raid the Russian base, killing everyone on sight. We were an unstoppable force, and we wiped out everyone. No one stood a chance. After we killed Devon, the Butcher Queen called her entire army to us, knowing what guns we had. We rushed into action.

El fin.

Xander Youngless

Hi! I'm Xander Youngless! I'm a WISH Academy High School student who enjoys monsters, horror, and folklore. I began making comics in the third grade, then fan fiction of the Diary of a Wimpy Kid books. However, I started making my own stories in the 6th grade and have ever since! When not scribbling on paper or on my computer, I watch horror movies at the New Beverly Cinema! This is my first-ever published story. It's called "The Scholomance."

This Scholmance is a school in Romanian folklore, located in Transylvania, where monsters go to learn their craft. But what happens when two monster HUNTERS try to sneak in to kill all the students in one fell swoop? WHO WILL STOP THEM!? Find out when you turn the page…

Tales of the Scholomance

by Xander Youngless

Oh! Phew.
So, Emi! I assume we are heading to the graveyard to kick monster butt?
No. Actually, we are going on a secret mission to...
The Scholomance.
Sorry, I wanted to do that for dramatic effect.

The Scholomance is a prestigious K-12 school for monster girls.
Sholomance literally means School of Magic in Latin and...
Wait, why are we here already?
Yay! New friends!
Becasue the creator of this comic is on a tight deadline.
Oh! Um...
MMPH!
Who are you?
Sh—
We are foreign exchange students. I come from Japan, and she comes from Where the Wild Things Are.
HEY!!
Well, come in! We're all friends down here!

And so, the Montage begins...
Science!
AAAA!
AAAA
History!
AAA
A AA
Math!
Ok, this isn't so bad...
OH, COME ON!

LUNCH!
There she is, Robin. Countess Bela, the VAMPIRE.
In the immortal words of Mortal Kombat, finish her!
Ok
Wooden Stake
- and then I raised my arms dramatically, like this!
SWEET LAMASUTU!
Sniff

Oh, crap.
She's choking!
Clatter
HERE! I'll help by doing the thing with the chest pressing!
Crunch!
Just play along.
Good! Keep doing the thing! I'll get the nurse-
Nicht so schnell!*
Ay?
*Not so fast!
I've noticed that this girl's fur smells of burnt plastic, meaning it's fake. That means...
Get off me!

RIP!
Gasp
This girl is a fraud!
Er... Wow. What a shocker.
Someone call M. Night Shyamalan...
Oh, she's a fraud too, BTW.
NOP
W-wait!
You filthy liars!
ZIP!
We're in a school anthology, remember?
Gore is not allowed!
You can't kill us!
Gosh darn it!
Hmmm...
HA HA HA HA

What'sss going on?
Slither...
We got a couple schmutzes back here. Can you petrify them?
Yess!! Besst day ever!!
NO!
G-GUChhhh!!!
That's gonna leave a mark!
Hey! It's OK! We'll just chisel the marks away!
Later...
So, that's why you were late today?
Yes, Mother. All true, too!
Suuuure. And WHERE are the statues?

Hehe he...
Oh ho ho, I can't wait until she sees the Scholomance gates tomorrow night...
Hmm hmm hmm...
Splish!
Paint
Stupid Human
Another Stupid Human
End!

Kiani Hodo

Kiani Hodo is a student at WISH Academy High School who enjoys writing fantasy stories and creating new worlds with her writing. She began writing in the seventh grade after a narrative assignment. When not writing, Kiani likes to code, draw, read, do math, play music, make music, fly drones, play video games, and learn about science. This is Kiani's first published story.

A Puppet's Last Dance
By Kiani Hodo

On the bisected planet Quavora, there were three main regions: the Upper World, the Lower World, and the Ring. The Upper World was closer in proximity to the star Quavora orbits, which is where light-based creatures known as Aereons reside. The Lower World is further away from the star, which makes it a great place for the shadow-based creatures, Zebilians, to live in. Finally, The Ring is where Xunarans, creatures with neither darkness nor light, live. Their leaders, Zacius and Seciri, are in control of both halves of the planet. They use puppets to enforce control over both lands, and this new design seems to be their best one yet.

Within the Ring…

A duo performs…

Their dance begins with production…

They gather the Ring's icy debris…

Creating the puppet's body…

Their dance continues with gracefulness…

They gather particles from each World…

Creating the puppet's sharp eyes and short hair…

Their dance moves on to strength…

They gather their energy…

Creating the puppet's skills and attacks…

Their dance concludes with the end product…

They gather the pieces and put them in place…

Creating their best puppet…

Her purpose on this planet…

Destroy all rebels…

Destroy all of the unworthy ones…
The duo's performance comes to a close…
Creating their strongest puppet…

Xhun…

Part 1

A few months later…

Today was Xhun's first time in the Upper World, where 99% of rebellions occurred. Zacius had ordered her to start her task within the center of the marketplace, where many possible rebels were hiding in plain sight. The marketplace was full of Aereons selling the strangest things, from clothes to foodstuffs to strange objects they found somewhere. This was the busiest time of the day, according to Zacius, so there were plenty of candidates for possible rebels.

LOCATING REBELS…Xhun's sensors scanned the passerby, checking for the **UNWORTHY** alarm to flash in her line of sight. So far… nothing. She kept looking around until she felt something bump into her. **IMPOSSIBLE** . Impossible. She turned around to see a light-blue Aereon step back in surprise. Xhun had never seen an Aereon with such an…aquatic color scheme. Her eyes were teal, and her long hair was all sorts of lavender and blue.

"Oh my goodness! I'm so sorry!" she exclaimed. "Are you okay?" She checked Xhun for any sign of injury, which was strange since puppets never get injured.

"Extremities unharmed," Xhun replied.

"That's good," the newcomer said. She held out her hand, which was glowing a little. "I'm Torai. What's your name?"

"Xhun."

"Do you want to be friends?"

??? Xhun's mind did not comprehend the idea of "friends," nor did she know what to say.

JUST SAY YES, Zacius's voice echoed in Xhun's mind. Trust me.

"Yes," Xhun said. "Yay!" Torai cheered. She grabbed Xhun's hand and led her through the marketplace. "We don't get many Xunarans to visit! I am so excited to show you around!"

Xhun did not know what to do with this…physical contact. Based on her observations, Xunarans don't hug. They don't hold hands. Some don't even have hands, just geometric concepts of hands. Xunarans don't hug, nor apologize for their actions. They just…exist. But this strange Aereon is being voluntarily friendly, and Xhun's sensors were uneasy with this new development.

As the two of them kept walking, Xhun noticed that Torai was leading her to a peaceful meadow. The flowers were a blend of colors, ranging from bright pink to the palest of lavenders. Each flower emitted light at different frequencies every once in a while, which awakened something in Xhun. **IS THIS CONSIDERED… PRETTY? AM I FINDING SOMETHING… PRETTY? AND I'M OKAY WITH THIS? WHAT IS THIS? WHAT'S GOING ON?**

Torai gazed upon the flowers and took a deep breath. "Do you feel it?" she asked.

"Feel what?" Xhun asked.

"The wind blowing on your face? The soft petals blowing in your hair? It's so relaxing."

"It is indeed windy."

Torai ushered Xhun to what she could only assume was the middle of this flowerbed and lay herself down. She beckoned for Xhun to lie down beside her. As Xhun copied Torai's movements, she felt the soft petals tickling her face, and the gentle breeze on her face. She didn't know what was happening to her, but she felt…comfortable. At ease. Her sensors weren't on high alert this time. They've seemed to die down a little bit. She looked at Torai's smiling face, and she felt the corners of her mouth turn upward.

"Aww, look at you! You're so cute when you smile!" Torai said happily. "Do other Xunarans smile? I am curious."

"Some don't have faces," Xhun countered. "I've never seen anyone show emotion." **WHY AM I TELLING HER THIS?** Xhun felt her mind short-circuit for a second. Puppets aren't supposed to tell anybody their business. Why was she sharing all of this with a stranger? Was it the strange feeling inside of her doing this? What is this?

Torai plucked a flower from the meadow and carefully placed it in Xhun's hair. It was a pale blue one, and it glowed a little. Its petals were large and full, and it almost covered one of Xhun's eyes, but Torai adjusted it so she could see.

"…Thank you," Xhun murmured. She felt her mouth curling upwards again. She could feel part of her mouth opening. She decided to copy the gesture and perfectly sliced a flower equivalent to hers off its stem. Then she carefully placed it in Torai's hair, making sure it was perfectly placed at a 45-degree angle near her temple. When she finished, she felt something akin to satisfaction.

"Thank you so much, Xhun!" Torai cheered. "I love it!"

"You're welcome," Xhun replied. She felt that strange emotion through her chest again. Something inside Torai was causing Xhunt to feel this way, and she did not know what this was. But…she enjoyed that feeling.

"Come on, let's find another fun place to go!" Torai said as she grabbed Xhun's hand and led her through the meadow. The two of them skipped and frolicked for what seemed like hours, and Xhun was loving it!

Interlude…

Meanwhile…

On the Ring, Zacius watched. He watched his puppet cavort around with some Aereon girl. He watched his best work fall down the drain. It fueled him with the utmost rage. No. He needed to calm down. Be patient. He needed to wait. He turned to his companion, Seciri, as she manipulated her power over the Lower World with ease. He knew that she was a master at control, something he strived to have for a long time.

He glided over to her and placed all four hands on her shoulders. "Seciri dear," he purred. "It seems like my new project is feeling…emotions. I don't know what to do with her."

Seciri turned to him and stared through that black veil of hers. "Then you should terminate the project, since she's so unworthy," she said coldly.

"But you know I love these puppets. And with time, I know she'll come to her senses."

"I know you have high hopes for this prototype, but you've made this one too independent. What if she turns on you?"

"She won't." Zacius held Seciri's hands in his and wrapped his other arms around her waist. He led her in a slow-paced dance. The two of them danced around the control tower for a long time. As the music reached a crescendo, he spun her around and dipped her.

"Trust me, dear. As long as I'm around, she will never turn on me," Zacius whispered as he lifted Seciri back up. As the music reached its end, he returned to his control station and watched his screen with an emotion that resembled glee and anticipation.

Part 2

Torai led Xhun to a nearby park where there was a quartet of musicians playing some sort of music, and others were dancing along to the sounds from the stringed instruments. Xhun noticed there were a lot of plants at this strange place, but they weren't nearly as pretty as the meadow Torai took her to. There were bushes and glowing trees, and there were some small critters scattered around the area.

Xhun wanted to observe everything, but Torai led her to the area where the musicians and dancers were gathered around.

"Come on! Let's dance! It'll be fun!" she said. She grabbed Xhun's hands and moved along with the music. Xhun noticed that the music was somewhat fast and it had a bit of a bounce(?) to it. As she listened to it, she felt her mouth curling upward again.

HOW DO I DANCE?

DON'T WORRY, Zacius's voice echoed inside Xhun's mind.

With that new knowledge, Xhun grabbed Torai's hands and led her through a dance. She made sure her moves were tight and precise. Torai's mouth curved upward in that word she called a smile as she joined in. Her movements were more fluid and carefree than Xhun's, but she didn't mind. She enjoyed having Torai around.

The music shifts to something similar to what it was before, but this time it has a stiffer bounce to it. Torai took the lead this time as she spun Xhun around. She made a sound that Xhun learned was called a laugh as the two of them spun each other all over the area. This new experience made Xhun feel like she and Torai were the only ones in the park, and she was loving it. But..

 Zacius cut in.

Xhun looked at Torai. She didn't see anything suspicious about her.

"Is something wrong, Xhun?" Torai asked. She looked so concerned for Xhun. Xhun's happy emotions went into overdrive. Over what? A stranger? Why did Zacius care so much —

The **UNWORTHY** alarm flashed in front of Xhun's face. Normally, when the alarm flashed that upper-case bolded word, it would be aquamarine. But this sign flashed a deep red, something that no puppet had ever seen before.

"Nothing's wrong," Xhun answered.

Torai's face melted in relief. "That's good. Also…" She leaned closer and smiled. "Thank you for being my new friend. I've never gotten to do this before with my other friends. They're not as fascinating as you are. You've been really fun!"

The music changed again. This time, it was slower-paced music that Xhun recognized. She would see Zacius and Seciri dance to music like this all the time. Torai took the lead again, and Xhun noticed how much concentration it took for Torai to try not to step on her feet.

WHAT ARE YOU WAITING FOR. XHUN? KILL HER

Something in Xhun's mind froze. She didn't know why, but something inside of her was refusing to commit to the action.

WHAT IS THIS? WHy *am I feeling this way? I… don't want to eliminate her.*

DO IT.

I-I can't

Suddenly, Torai wrapped her arms around Xhun in a nice and gentle hug. "Let's be best friends, alright?"

"Okay," Xhun murmured. *I feel happy around this new…friend!*

AS YOUR PUPPET MASTER. I COMMAND YOU TO ELIMINATE THIS ONE. SHE IS UNWORTHY OF STAYING IN MY PERFECT WORLD.

Xhun looked down for a moment, and the music began to pick up in tempo. She looked Torai dead in the eye…and took the lead.

One-two-three

One-two-three

Spin-two-three

Step-two-three

Pivot-two-three
Turn-two-three
Glide-two-three
FADE!

TWO!

BLACK!

SLASH! *-two-three*

SPIN! *-two-three*

ATTACK! *-two-three*

*one-two-*SLASH!

Pivot- ATTACK! *-three*

SLASH! *-two-three*

*Dip-two-*SLASH!

One-two-three

One- **SLASH! SLASH!**

ATTACK! *-two-three*

Step-step- **SLASH!**

Spin-two-three

Step-Step-three

Step-step- **SLASH!**

FIN–ISH–IT!

One-two-three

One-two-three

Fade-back-three

When Xhun finished the dance, she looked at what was left of her friend. There were so many pitch-black wounds, and they were so deep. She felt a strange liquid run down her face. She felt it in her eyes. Everything was blurry, her sensors were overwhelmed, and her heart was filled with strange emotions.
But she did hear this: "That puppet killed the princess!!"
"Avenge the princess! Kill the puppet!" someone else yelled. Soon, an entire mob of Aereons ran and flew towards her. Xhun didn't know what to do with herself, but the **UNWORTHY** alarm was blaring through her mind, so she had to obey her orders.

One attacker? Done.

Someone attacks above her head? Done.

Another attacker? Done.

Someone who threw an explosive at her? Done.

UNWORTHY? Done.

UNWORTHY? Destroyed.

UNWORTHY? Decimated.

UNWORTHY? Annihilated.

UNWORTHY? Assassinated.

UNWORTHY? All gone.

It was a massacre...

Xhun stared at the bodies in front of her, and she felt the liquid from her eyes again. It aggressively ran down her face in streams. She felt her shoulders quaking as she fell to her knees and stared at the bodies beside her. She felt a strange feeling in her heart, but the emotion associated with it was very gloomy.

A portal shattered open, and Zacius stepped through it. He was much taller than Xhun, and he picked her up and held her with all four arms. He walked through the portal, leading them back to the Ring.

Zacius set Xhun down facing him and placed his hands on her shoulders.

"You poor little thing," he said.

"You're crying."

IS THAT WHAT'S GOING ON WITH ME? WHY?

"I CAN'T HAVE THAT." Zacius placed his hands on Xhun's head and spoke within her mind.

WITH THESE HANDS

I SHALL FIX MY PUPPET

THIS ONE CAN NOT CHANGE

SHE SHALL CARRY OUT THE XUNARAN WILL:

NO MERCY

NO BONDING

NO ATTACHMENTS

WITH THIS CHANGE COMING TO A CLOSE

I SHALL CREATE MY MOST POWERFUL PUPPET YET

MY HEARTLESS KILLER XHUN...

The End

Veronica

Veronica is a student at WISH Academy High School who enjoys fictional novels, adventurous themes, and creative writing. She began writing after Ms. Avalos had encouraged her to try something new and venture out of her comfort zone. When not writing, Veronica likes to draw, watch movies, and shows. This is her first published story.

From Enemies to Friends
by Veronica

Vanessa has always been the pretty, smart girl in class, but school didn't always come easy. Vanessa is a 15-year-old brown-skinned girl with long curly brown hair. She currently attends a high school in her small town in Georgia. But academics were never the issue. Excelling in her AP classes was easy enough for her, although for once, she wanted to be recognized for something other than her smarts.

"Good morning!" Vanessa greets Melanie with a smile.

Melanie rolls her eyes and continues to walk.

It was obvious why other girls didn't like her. She was beautiful. Although many envied her hazel brown eyes, there was one who seemed to despise Vanessa. She made it her mission to overpass Vanessa in every way possible. That girl was Melanie.

"Vanessa may be better at math, but at least I'm a better volleyball player," Melanie thinks to herself walking to her next class.

Although Melanie may shoot snarky looks at Vanessa here and there, she never seemed to have a true hatred for her. Nevertheless, Vanessa seemed to ignore her immaturity. She had better things to worry about… like summer break!

"I can't wait for summer break! We have about two weeks left," Vanessa exclaims.

"We should go somewhere! I'm thinking of a trip to Florida!" Leilani, Vanessa's friend, shares. They all nod in agreement imagining how fun the next couple of months will be. But for now, Vanessa needed to focus on finals, and the thing holding her down the most, volleyball.

Volleyball had been a love-hate relationship with Vanessa. Although she loved the sport, she didn't like the competition that comes with it. Volleyball made her feel less than compared to other girls on the JV team which to Vanessa was a foreign feeling. Vanessa was used to always being the top in her class. But this gave Vanessa nothing but motivation for the next season. "Meet at my house after school?" Kylie asks the friend group.

"Sure," They all agree in unison.

"Well, I'm kinda busy," Vanessa hesitantly states. "I've been feeling this weight on my shoulder because of volleyball. Sorry guys, but I'll be practicing tonight," she sighs. As weeks passed by, Vanessa's training intensified. She was looking forward to the break. "*Thank goodness it's the last day of school,*" Vanessa thinks to herself.

"Morning," Melanie smirks.

"Good morning," Vanessa replied, analyzing the insincere greeting.

"You ready for tryouts? I heard it's starting early this year."

Vanessa thinks to herself wondering what Melanie could be possibly planning this time.

Little did she know, Melanie wasn't trying to tease her but genuinely remind her. "I mean, I've been practicing to improve my skills, and who knows maybe I'll become team captain of the girl's JV volleyball team!"

"Whatever you say I guess," Melanie sarcastically rolls her eyes.

"What could she have possibly meant by 'whatever you say'?" Vanessa couldn't stop replaying that moment in her head.

It seemed obvious to Vanessa that Melanie was trying to get to her head, but this time, she made sure it wasn't going to work.

BING! Vanessa's phone vibrated.

As a couple of months passed Vanessa had gotten so caught up with volleyball that she had forgotten about her own friends!

We still up for Florida? Leilani texted the group chat.

Yup! Both Kylie and Jessica replied.

Vanessa contemplated before saying anything. She didn't want to risk anything that could ruin her chances of becoming captain. Eventually, she concluded that she was being too hard on herself and she didn't want to miss out on spending quality time with her friends. "*Okay, send the time and place and I'll be there,*" Vanessa texts back.

"*Tmrw our flight's at 5, but first meet at my house by 3,*" Leilani asserts to everyone.

"*Got it!*" Jessica mentions.

They met according to the plan and as they reached the airport, Vanessa's mind had been completely taken off the stress.

"Guys wake up we've arrived!" Leilani shouts in excitement.

Vanessa woke up to a bright ray of sunshine through the plane window. The next couple of days were the most fun Vanessa had experienced all year. They explored beaches and went to Disney World. But as the trip came to an end, school was about to begin. As soon as Vanessa got back to her hometown, she began buying the supplies she would need for her favorite classes. Vanessa was feeling good about everything. That was until she walked past the sporting section.

"TRYOUTS!" Vanessa screamed in terror.

She rushed through her emails checking to see the dates of when tryouts were scheduled. Hoping to see that she hadn't missed them during her vacation.

"What?! No way, this can't be true," Vanessa cried in denial.

She missed what she desperately worked so hard for. To prove to coaches that she would be good enough to instruct her team. But instead, now she wasn't even on a team. Vanessa felt nothing but despair.

School begins bright and early at 8:00 am and Vanessa is now a Junior in high school. These were all things that would usually bring her joy, but Vanessa didn't care this year.

"Even Melanie tried to tell me," she murmured to herself.

Vanessa tried everything to get back on the team. Emailing coaches, talking to them in person, and even promoting her skills on her Instagram. Yet, nothing.

"What's up with you? Not like I care or anything," Melanie asks after noticing Vanessa's bright smile is gone.

"I missed it. Even you tried to tell me," She faintly replied feeling ashamed of herself. Normally, this would've been the highlight of Melanie's year. She would have no one to compete with, and Vanessa would be out of her sight! But for some odd reason, Melanie didn't feel satisfied, for the first time, she felt bad.

"Yeah well, I'll see you in the fifth period," Melanie said.

"Right," Vanessa replied.

Instead of Melanie going on about her day, she wanted to help Vanessa. Even if the thought of that wanted to make her throw up.

"Coach M, I know she missed tryouts but I think she could truly help make the team," Melanie tries to convince.

"Well, she missed both dates. We even had make-up tryouts," Coach responded. "Please, I know Vanessa worked hard on improving her skills to make the team," Melanie couldn't believe the words coming out of her mouth.

"I'll see what I can do," Coach let out a big sigh.

Melanie smiled from ear to ear knowing that it was a yes coming from Coach M, the stubbornest volleyball coach there is. To Vanessa, the first couple of weeks felt like school was just another burden. That was until she received an email from…

"COACH M?" Vanessa screamed with her whole chest. She was so eager she almost forgot to read the email!

"*A recommendation sparked my eyes and after days of consideration, and through searching your social platforms, I believe that you would make a great captain for our girl's Varsity volleyball team*," the email stated.

"I MADE THE VARSITY TEAM!" Vanessa's heart nearly pounded out of her chest as she jumped up and announced to all of her friends in the group chat.

"Wait, a recommendation from who?" she pondered.

She thought back to how Melanie came late to the fifth period which she never had because English had always been her favorite subject. Not only that, but she recalled seeing Melanie talk to the volleyball coach. Her smile grew in disbelief knowing that her so-called "enemy" wanted what was best for her. The next day rolled around and Vanessa knew the first thing she was going to do.

"Hey, Melanie! I just wanted to say thanks!" Vanessa warm-heartedly announced.

"Oh, it's nothing," Melanie shyly let out a smile. But this time, it felt sincere. Vanessa felt like Melanie was the closest friend she ever had.

Melanie smiled from ear to ear knowing that it was a yes coming from Coach M, the stubbornest volleyball coach there is. To Vanessa, the first couple of weeks felt like school was just another burden. That was until she received an email from…

"COACH M?" Vanessa screamed with her whole chest. She was so eager she almost forgot to read the email!

"*A recommendation sparked my eyes and after days of consideration, and through searching your social platforms, I believe that you would make a great captain for our girl's Varsity volleyball team,*" the email stated.

"I MADE THE VARSITY TEAM!" Vanessa's heart nearly pounded out of her chest as she jumped up and announced to all of her friends in the group chat.

"Wait, a recommendation from who?" she pondered.

She thought back to how Melanie came late to the fifth period which she never had because English had always been her favorite subject. Not only that, but she recalled seeing Melanie talk to the volleyball coach. Her smile grew in disbelief knowing that her so-called "enemy" wanted what was best for her. The next day rolled around and Vanessa knew the first thing she was going to do.

"Hey, Melanie! I just wanted to say thanks!" Vanessa warm-heartedly announced.

"Oh, it's nothing," Melanie shyly let out a smile. But this time, it felt sincere. Vanessa felt like Melanie was the closest friend she ever had.

"Wanna hang out after school?" Vanessa nervously asked.

"Definitely!" Melanie replied within an instant.

For once, it didn't feel like a competition between the two of them. It just felt like a genuine friendship.

Philip Speer

Philip Speer is a student at WISH Academy High School who enjoys action books, writing fantasy, adventure stories, and exploring human emotions through fiction, while crafting tales inspired by history. He began writing after taking Ms. Avalos' English class where she assigned an assignment for writing a book, which inspired me to make more. When not writing, Philip likes to play video games. This is his first published story.

The Adventure of Blackeye Gringlebeard
by Philip Speer

In Pirateland, everyone was a pirate. It was a place filled with swashbucklers and thievery. However, not everyone was happy in Pirateland. Like Blackeye Gringlebeard. He was tall, with a thick beard, and an eye patch over his left eye. But, most importantly, Blackeye didn't want to be a pirate. He hated it. But he had to. There was no choice in Pirateland.

But one day, Blackeye had enough. He was going to leave Pirateland and never come back. He was wasting his life doing nothing. So he gathered up all his stuff and left for the docks. When he got there, he heard a loud voice, stopping him where he stood.

"Where are you going, Gringlebeard?"

Blackeye whipped around and saw Captain Pirateguy, the vicious leader of every pirate living in Pirateland. Blackeye's heart beat faster, but he stood his ground. "I'm leaving," Blackeye said, a bit scared.

Pirateguy walked closer. "Not so fast, Gringlebeard. You aren't leaving Pirateland. Nobody is. Not while I'm the captain."

With a snap of his fingers, Captain Pirateguy summoned five men and ordered them to arrest Blackeye. But he was able to fight them off.

"No traitor is going to ruin my 30th anniversary day as leader. I'll take you in myself," said the Captain.

With a whack so quick that Blackeye couldn't even see it, Captain Pirateguy hit him in the head with the butt of his pistol. Blackeye was immediately knocked out cold. Blackeye jolted awake and looked around. "Where am I," he muttered. He hadn't woken up fully yet.

Blackeye was in a dark, cold jail cell. It smelled horrible. The only light coming into his cell was from a torch in the hallway outside and a bit of moonlight from a window. He heard music and chanting in the distance. That must be from the celebration of the captain's 30th year of leadership. Everyone was there.

Blackeye looked out into the hallway, desperately searching for something to help him escape. To his surprise, he saw someone he'd known his entire life. His childhood friend Joe. This gave Blackeye an idea.

"Joe," Blackeye whispered. "Joe it's me, Blackeye. I need your help."

He hesitated, but came over. "I can't let you go. If Captain Pirateguy finds out he'll lock me up too, or worse…"

"He won't find out I promise. Please, help me. I have to escape. I can't be a pirate anymore. We can both escape this island on my boat."

Joe finally agreed. He unlocked Blackeye's cell and they both slipped out.

Sneaking in the darkness past the loud tavern, they made their way over to the dock.

There it was. Blackeye's ship. The Isaacson. It was big and long and beautiful.

"HEY YOU! STOP!"

Unfortunately for Blackeye and Joe, not everyone was at the celebration. There were two guards at the dock, and they had spotted them. Blackeye and Joe charged them. They killed the first, but the second escaped. While he was running towards the tavern to warn the others, he threw a bomb at the Isaacson. It blew up in a huge explosion and immediately sank. "Now what?" Joe asked in a panic.

Blackeye looked around for another way out, and then he saw it. Captain Pirateguy's ship, The Big One. It was a huge ship. Too big for just two pirates to operate. But they'd have to. "We'll take Captain Pirateguy's ship, The Big One. Quick, get on!"

Blackeye and Joe rushed onto the ship and began preparing it to set sail. But in the distance, they heard a crowd of pirates running towards them. The guard had alerted the others of the escape! The two hurried to raise the sails before the mob got to them.

Just as the mob reached them, Blackeye and Joe raised the anchor and began sailing away. But, with pirates, it's never that simple.

"You think you can escape me, Gringlebeard? I'll show you what happens to traitors!" Captain Pirateguy had leapt onto the boat at the last second. He drew his sword and began attacking Blackeye and Joe.

The pair of pirates drew their swords as well and fought back as hard as they could. But they soon realized that they were no match for the Captain. Joe looked at Blackeye with an odd look in his eyes.

"Goodbye, friend," Joe whispered. He charged full force at Pirateguy, knocking both the Captain and himself overboard.

"NOOOOO!" Blackeye yelled out to his friend. He rushed over to the side of the boat and looked over the edge, but neither Joe or the captain were there. They had been pulled under the waves, never to be seen again.

Blackeye was heartbroken. His childhood friend had given his life for Blackeye to have his freedom. At this exact moment, Blackeye vowed for his friend's sacrifice to not be in vain. He would honor his friend's memory by living his life and enjoying his freedom. Blackeye Gringlebeard sailed away, never looking back, escaping Pirateland forever.

Analise Tessema

Analise Tessema is a student at WISH Academy High School who enjoys mysterious magical realism and speculative fiction that explores themes of mortality and what it means to be human. She began writing in 1st grade, "I have always wanted to make a story I can truly enjoy and that makes me think, even when playing with dolls or making comics. I suppose that is why I started writing, to satisfy my and hopefully other's desire for this as well", she says. This is her first published story!

The Paws of the Beholder
by Analise Tesseman

After coming home from her date, Janice felt nauseous. To be fair, this happened every time she came home from a date with her boyfriend. Once she got home, everything felt too "real".

"Janice, are you okay?" a sweet voice said from across the hallway, spooking Janice, who didn't "sneak" out of the bathroom very well.

"I'm fine, I just probably ate something I'm allergic to," Janice responded as she wiped the saliva from her mouth.

"Janice, if that's true, don't go on your date tomorrow."

"Tomorrow?"

"Janice, the light show- You-", Mrs. Kim massaged her temple while muttering something in Korean.

"I'm sorry, I probably forgot."

"Janice, I just don't want you to do something you don't want to do, alright."

"Mom, I'll think about it."

"Janice, I'm serious."

"I know."

"Alright." Mrs. Kim marched to Janice and gave her a peck on her forehead, then marched back to the bedroom. "Good Night, Janice."

"Good Night, Mom," Janice responded, and she felt a pit grow in her stomach. She needed to sleep this off. Straight down the other side of the hall, Janice slipped through her room and threw herself on her bed and sank in. Janice sometimes wished she could drown in it, but the last time she tried to, she realized how painful it was and never did it again. It's not like the temptation was never there, though.

Crawling to the other side of her bed, pressing the on button of her lamp, it glowed a warm yellow, its hue warming her soul. Janice plucked her phone out of the side pocket of her romper and plugged her phone into its charger. She needed to clean up, but her bathroom felt as far as someone's room could feel. Groaning, Janice sat up and lazily gazed around her room filled with her trinkets, plushies, figures, and posters that, if anyone from her school saw, she would never leave her house again. Janice's gaze continues until her eyes cling to her desk, or what was atop it. It was a plush toy Elle had gotten for her, its rotund tummy looked incredibly soft and plush. Janice would have cuddled with it to bed if it wasn't for its eyes; imitating tapioca, its beady eyes were cute, but it felt as if it were always watching you. As Janice moved her head from side to side, its eyes seemed to follow contentedly. She hoped Elle thought this was creepy in a cute way and not just.

"*Cute!*"

The little sound of Elle's voice made Janice smile. Elle always finds the weirdest thing to give her. Janice, rising from her seat on the bed, toured her collection of gifts from Elle around her room. The sculptures, books, and jewelry that Janice fell in love with the second time Elle presented them to her. One particular gift stood out to her: violets made from plastic bricks. Elle loved violets, which made Janice like violets a bit more. Elle always wore earrings that had violets on them. When Janice asked her why, she always said, "It is a symbol of love and connection". Janice could always tell it was something more than that, but if Elle didn't want to say, she wouldn't push it. Janice caressed the hard, shiny petals with her nail, Violets reminded her of Elle, and God, she needed Elle right now. Janice sighed and waltzed into her bathroom.

Maybe Elle and I could get matching earrings, This thought made Janice's cheeks feel unusually hot. It was so silly.

It's just earrings
Janice closes the door.
They don't mean that much
she turns the shower's knob to warm
But to Elle, it could mean a lot
she undresses
I wonder if Elle would like it

That thought made her cheeks feel hot, watching her body flush. What the hell was wrong with her? Janice climbed into the shower swiftly, nearly slipping on the wet marble floor while attempting to plant her feet on the mat. Promptly sliding the door closed once she regained her balance.

Maybe because of the door or the shower volume, Janice couldn't hear the shuffling of papers and appliances on her desk. A shadow stretched and curved as its tail slowly swung side to side. Descending from the desk, she took in the room's warm atmosphere, the sweet smell of candles and body mist was a proper welcome for someone of her status. Her tail curved slightly, curling near its tip before jumping near the end of Janice's bed. The girl was the first one on her list and had made a good impression. "It's a shame", her honeyed voice chirped as she kneaded at the long pillow that would soon be her perch. She extends a paw, protracting and retracting. It's always good to warm up before you exert your powers. "I can only hope she lasts longer than the other one."

"Yo! JANICE!" Beau's booming voice grabbed her attention at the top of a staircase behind her.

"Oh my god, Beau there are other people here shut up!"

"She literally passed us and didn't see us, I was just trying to get her attention."

"And the attention of every other person here!"

In front of a white gazebo, Elle appeared behind Beau, attempting to strangle him from his back collar while lecturing him. Elle and Beau are siblings, so Janice has known him for as long as she's known Elle. Even if Janice and he weren't close, he was always kind to her and Elle, regardless of how mean his sister was to him. Even while being strangled by Elle he wasn't fighting back just tapping out with his right hand so he wouldn't drop the plastic grocery bag he was holding in his left.

The plan was to have hot cocoa as they watched the light show, and everyone would bring the required ingredients and a little something extra. Elle and Beau brought Dark chocolate hot cocoa powder that seemed to be a special or luxury mix from a chocolate brand, an electric pot, and what appeared to be homemade peppermint stirring sticks. The confection display emanates the thought they put into this plan, making Janice a little jealous. Beau had always been good at making desserts and Elle always found cool stuff none had seen before. But it was hard not to be a little envious as before Janice was heavy cream, almond milk, and two bars of chocolate. All they were missing were marshmallows, whipped cream, and Andrew, Janice's boyfriend. And it was beginning to wear on everyone's patience, especially Janice. "Janice, do you know where he is?"

"He said he'd be here in 10 minutes, Beau", Janice responded.

Andrew's tardiness was a poor habit of his, but Janice had hoped he would try to come at least on time.

Tessema 3

Janice groaned as she drooped down to the table, visibly exhausted. Every year during the second week of December, the city hosts a Christmas light show at the pier. Boats are decorated with lights and dance on them wearing festive costumes whilst throwing candy at the dazzled spectators. Janice had been before with Elle and Beau, but when mentioning it off-handedly to Andrew he asked if he could attend with them. She had initially felt offended at the proposition that he come along, but there was no good reason to say no or to admit that she didn't want to attend. Especially for the finale, the fireworks.

"Whatever, let's just make the cocoa," Elle started as she tied up her locks in a loose bun above her head and rolled up her sleeves.

"But Janice's boyfriend isn't here yet"

"We can bring him some, remember we have a thermos in the bag."

Janice felt a light touch on the top of her head, drawing her to face Elle's warm gaze. "C'mon Janice, get up," Elle whispered.

The whisper was so low barley Janice could hear it, but she heard it regardless and it propelled her up with her cheeks flushed and ears ringing as she grabbed her items and walked across the long white table and placed her ingredients with theirs. Andrew could wait, right now Elle wanted Janice to make hot cocoa with her.

While Beau made the cocoa, Janice and Elle were in charge of mixing and pouring the steaming fluid into the thermos flasks the sibling brought. Beau would be trying his hand at French hot chocolate, thanks to Janice. The siblings made it clear how grateful they were for the heavy cream and milk. But, Janice had known for a while that Elle wanted to try french hot chocolate and was lactose-intolerant. Elle is gonna love this, Janice fantasized.

That fantasy became a reality to Janice and very much Elle's delight and as they carefully poured the cocoa into the thermos' Elle and Janice conversed.

"So Janice, how are you and Andrew."

"Yeah, yeah, uhh.. We're good I'm just worried."

Janice pauses as she pours some cocoa into a flask.

"What do you mean?"

"I just don't think he's the one."

"There is no guarantee that the person you date in high school will be your soulmate." Elle finishes filling the flask with cocoa.

"Yeah and I- just- this relationship makes me feel drained" Janice starts to pour into her flask lightly.

"No relationship should make you feel like that, it should make you happy and energetic, ya know. Someone you would be willing to spend the rest of your life listening to them yap about stuff they like."

Elle rests her chin the the palm of her hand as she leans on the table.

"Like a best friend?" Janice responded.

Elle's tan skin light like a red light bulb. She covered her mouth as well as refusing to look back at Janice. At that moment Janice noticed that Elle was wearing the violet earrings, her eyes glowing more than the last time she had seen her.

"By that logic Elle, I wouldn't mind if I had to marry you"

Wait, what the hell did I just say?

Janice jumped back, the cocoa's open flask spilling onto the wooden panels of the seat, falling backward onto the floor.

"I didn't mean it like that!" Janice refuted, her hands moving wildly.

"No, uh- I know," Elle responded her voice soaked in discomfort as well as amusement. As funny as Elle may have perceived it, Janice felt as if she just spilled her literal guts.

"Uh, I'll be right back." Janice hastily walked out the exit the into a small clearing behind the gazebo, Beau and Elle watching her go. She could feel their concern as she exited.

What was wrong with her? Why did that joke bother her so much? It's just Elle, why would she even care about marrying her?

The thought of that possibility made Janice feel sweaty and caused her heart to race.

It's not like I want to marry Elle, that's ridiculous.
Even if I was into girls there is no way she would like me back. Oh my
God! What is wrong with me?

Suddenly it became quiet, Janice couldn't hear the sound of the ocean's waves, or the wind blowing the laves, nor the noises of Beau and Elle fighting. It was weird, too weird.

"I see honesty is not your specialty, Janice Kim", a voice as sweet and smooth as honey rises.

Janice attempts to turn to meet the owner of this voice, but it echoes and rings everywhere intensely. Just the sound of the voice makes throbs throughout Janice's head throb, dragging her to the floor. Small steps are taken by even smaller paws. Her cankles rounded her legs into the shape of spam musubi. While her form seemed cute and welcoming, her eyes were colder than the water surrounding the pier nearby.

"Who are you, and please stop!" Janice begged and writhed on the floor.

"I am your judge, jury, and executioner. You may call me whatever you desire." Her stout plump frame emerged from the brush in front of Janice. Her paw stretched upon Janice's knee. Janice peeked through the layers of her hair, which provided a veil in front of the cat. Janice almost screamed at what she saw, it was the plushie from her room.

"I will address myself with a fitting name that a girl of your stature.", she started as her dark eyes peered past Janice's hair to make eye contact with Janice.

"I am Tapioca, and I am here to kill you, Janice Kim"

Etienne

Etienne is a student at WISH Academy High School who enjoys expressing her innermost thoughts through literature. She began writing during the pandemic as an outlet for the solitude she felt. When not writing, Etienne likes to sing, act, write, and much more. This is her first published poem.

That's What I'd Like To Think
by Etienne

I had you, Then I didn't, or that's what I'd like to think
Because of course how long you'd stay was never set in ink
I'd thought about losing you time and time before
Though, nothing could prepare me for the day you didn't come
back through that door
I felt sad and betrayed, then mad at the world I wished it would
sit still while my mind unfurled
I learned little ways to cope, within due time
The fact was you reached the end of your path and I'm still on
mine
There are many times I wonder if you'd be proud
Like when I'm up there performing and singing aloud
There are some nights i sit in fear of the end
But it makes me less scared knowing I'll see you my friend
For the day that I see you again I'll be tickled pink
Because I had you, Then I didn't, or that's what I'd like to think.

Luc D'Arceaux

Luc D'Arceaux is a student at WISH Academy High School who enjoys Nonfiction and Historical Fiction. When not writing, Luc likes to paint, draw, sew, and do anything involving crafts. This is his first published story.

A New Symphony
by Luc D'Arceaux

Since I was a little girl, music has been a significant part of my life. I would listen to my mother play the piano and its dancing keys, watch musicians on television, and learn to play myself. By the age of seven, my talent was comparable to that of adults. I felt blessed to possess the gift of musicality, and my parents were determined to ensure I was always the best. However, when I was younger, I didn't fully understand how hard my parents would push me to excel in music. I loved it—up until recently. I just finished my sophomore year at a visual and performing art school focused on music. After school, I attend even more music classes. It's stressful, but my parents insist that I need this dedication to become the best pianist I can be. Lately, though, I've been feeling a bit lost in my passion for music. It's not that I don't want to play; I've just been getting distracted. I've even been lying to my parents for weeks now.

"Hi, Stella! How did your piano practice go?" my mom asked as I walked into the house.

"Oh, hey, Mom. It went well. We were just uhh working on perfecting a song I've been learning," I mumbled.

"Oh, alright. I'm cooking your favorite for dinner, so make sure to start on your homework now, so you don't have to do it later," she replied in a dull tone.

My mom hasn't been the same since a big fight with my dad, who isn't really in the picture anymore, and he isn't a legal guardian for me anymore. I don't even know why they were fighting, but it's not my place to know. I feel like I just have to put in my best effort because I don't want my mom to feel any worse. That's why I can't bring myself to tell her that I haven't been attending my after-school piano lessons for the past week.

I told myself that I would only skip one day of piano lessons to attend my friend Asha's art show. She had some of her paintings on display at a local gallery, and I must say, she's incredibly talented. Her paintings look like waves moving and water flowing; they are so artistic. This experience inspired me to start drawing for fun. However, I quickly found myself immersed in researching the world of art—painting, drawing, sculpting, everything. As a result, I ended up skipping piano lessons for the rest of that week to join Asha at the art studio she attends.

"You know, Stella, you really shouldn't lie to your mom," Asha said worryingly. "I get it, but she would freak out. Plus, you're the best piano player I know. You have to start going again."

"Yeah, I know," I replied. "But recently, I just haven't been able to play very well, and I'm losing interest. I can't afford to lose interest in piano; it's my life. But I wanna get more into art, especially painting. Do you know anyone who could teach me techniques or something?"

Yeah, I have a friend, maybe this weekend if you come to the studio my friend Max can kinda teach you some techniques!" Asha said excitedly.

It was Monday, and I had said I was going to start going to piano lessons again. However, I needed an excuse for missing an entire week. I was so scared to go that I felt like my heart was going to come out of my chest and explode. All I could think about was whether my piano instructor would be understanding and not tell my mother that I had missed a whole week. This worry consumed me at school, and even in music class, I couldn't focus. I had to step out of class because I was so stressed.

To make matters worse, my school was about to have its beginning-of-the-year concert, where I would be playing the piano. I was just thankful that the school day was finally over, as I needed to go to piano lessons and get back on track.

As I was walking out of school with my friend from band class, Sidney, she looked at me and asked, "Are you okay, Stella? You look a little off today."

"Ugh, yeah, I'm fine. I was just supposed to go to my after-school piano lessons, but I didn't go for a week, and my mom doesn't know that—Oh my god!" I exclaimed in fright.

"What??" Sidney replied, confused.

"My mom is standing right there! What the hell is she doing here? I have to go, okay? Bye!" I hurried over to my mom, who was standing outside her car. I was so confused. Why was she here?

"Uh, hey Mom, what are you doing here?" I asked, feeling anxious.

"What do you mean? I got the email that it was your check-in day at piano lessons, so I took the day off work to take you. I'm excited to see what you've been learning," my mom exclaimed.

"Oh, yeah, sorry, I just forgot about that…" I mumbled.

I was in a state of shock. I had no one to blame but myself—after all, that's what I get for skippi with you? Get it together," my mom said firmly.

"Sorry, I'm just stressed about everything right now. With school and piano…" I admitted anxiously.

"Well, maybe I can transfer you to a full music school," my mom suggested. "I don't want you to feel stressed, and I want you to have more time for practicing."

"Maybe…" I mumbled, unsure. Oh my god! My mom has a totally different idea of me. I just shouldn't have kept this secret for so long. I felt like a volcano about to burst. I couldn't handle this!

When we arrived at my lessons, my instructor greeted us. "Hey, Stella, and Ms. Davidson! Long time no see! It's been a week since I last saw you." I knew those words were coming, and a ringing filled my ears as I turned crimson.

"What do you mean? Stella told me she was here yesterday!" my mom questioned.

"Uh, nope! Yeah, Stella wasn't here yesterday…" My piano teacher Mr. R said.

Oh crap… Oh crap…

"Stella, what do you mean you weren't here" My mom questioned

"I… I don't know. I just… uhh," I muttered. I couldn't feel my feet. This was my worst nightmare. Piano was supposed to be my whole life—it was all I did! I couldn't even speak as tears started to stream down my face. I wanted my mom to understand and support my decision to stop playing piano, but I knew that would never happen.

I glanced over at my mom; she looked like she was about to explode. Her face was turning red, and the veins on her forehead were popping out. "Stella, what are you talking about? How could you lie to me? How could you do this?"

"Mom, please stop—"

"Don't tell me to stop! You need to explain yourself! I'm so sorry, Mr. R. I will deal with her…" my mom yelled angrily.

"No problem. Please give me a call later." He replied.

"Stella, we're leaving," my mom said, her voice tight with tension. I followed her quietly, anxiety swirling in my stomach, not wanting to escalate the situation. The elevator ride down felt like an eternity of silence, my mom's disappointed expression cutting deeper than any words she could have said. As tears went down my cheeks, I caught her glancing at me, confusion mingling with frustration.

"Why are you crying? This is your fault. I shouldn't feel sympathy for your mistakes," she snapped. I knew, deep down, that it was time to share the truth weighing on my heart. I didn't want to play the piano anymore. The pressure of being labeled a prodigy was suffocating. I yearned to explore different forms of art, to be free from it, unconfined by expectations.

"Mom, please just listen. I don't want to play the piano anymore! It's too much stress for me," I stammered, my voice shaky.

"What? I thought this was your passion. Why did you lie to me? If you didn't want to play, why didn't you tell me sooner? You're throwing away a gift!" she shouted, disbelief etched across her face.

"I think you're being unreasonable. You love the piano. You're going to quit just to dabble in other interests?"

"I just want to explore new passions! I've been diving into art lately, and it feels so liberating. I realize I'm talented at piano, but it's not bringing me joy anymore. I need a change." I replied, desperation creeping into my voice. I just felt deep down that my mom wouldn't care, she wouldn't understand the stress that comes with being labeled as a child prodigy. I just accepted my fate that I would have to play piano for the rest of my life.

"Well if that's what you want. But I'm still disappointed that you want to throw away something you've done all your life just for stuff you've never done. And I'm not saying I won't support you through this new journey of your life, but I will always be disappointed." My mom sadly muttered.

 "I understand, and I kept this secret from you because I didn't want to hurt you, but If I kept it any longer, I would have started to hurt myself." I sniffled, wiping my tears away.

Wow… I thought that this would go way differently. I felt like there were butterflies in my stomach flying away. I felt safe, and glad I was going to be able to be happier, find my new identity in whatever I wanted to do, and not be defined by a label I had since I was 7 years old.

"Thank you," I said to my mom as we hugged.

It's hard to believe that it's been a year since I decided to shift my focus away from music, my number one priority. Looking back, I realize how much my life revolved around school and music, creating a routine that was rewarding yet stressful. I often felt overwhelmed, as I juggled the demands of life along with the pressures of mastering musical skills. Now, I can say that I'm enrolled in the visual arts program at my school. This new journey has been incredibly transformative and more eventful than any other period of my life. In this environment, I can explore my artistic abilities in ways that I never imagined before. It has opened my eyes to different forms of expression and allowed me to connect with my friends who share similar passions.

Although I have stepped back from prioritizing music, I still play. However, I have shifted my focus to jazz. I find jazz to be liberating, as it encourages personal expression. Unlike structured musical forms like I was taught by, jazz allows me to break free from the rules and express my thoughts and feelings. It has become an outlet for me, offering a refreshing escape from the everyday reality I once found so constraining. As I navigate this new phase of my life, I continue to explore various experiences, embracing opportunities that come my way. Every day brings something new, whether it's discovering a new technique in my art classes, meeting inspiring individuals, or reflecting on my personal growth. I have learned to celebrate all my achievements, no matter how small, and to appreciate the journey itself. This year has taught me the value of balance and self-expression, and I eagerly look forward to what lies ahead.

Bowie Lamkin

Bowie Lamkin is a student at WISH Academy High School who enjoys writing stories based on movies. He began writing when he was influenced by his mom at 10. When not writing, Bowie likes to bake and watch movies. This is his first published story.

Takedown Takeover
by Bowie Lamkin

Zoning in and out on the wheel, he had been driving for days, just trying to reach his destination and end this. "They started it, I need to end it." He said. On the side of the road was a sign, 2 miles to Las Vegas. He is a known assassin by the name of Paul, trained by the most famous ninja ever, "The Hidden Blade". Many years ago Paul got injured in a fight and hasn't worked since. There is a yearning to go back but the perfection his mentor instilled in him tells him he couldn't do it anymore, so he never went back.

The reason Paul is driving is because of what happened 4 days ago. He was enjoying a weekend sitting down on his couch with all his favorite snacks. Randomly the tv glitched and switched to a live coverage feed of the owner of K.R Enterprises, Roman Pond, talking to the camera.

"This does not seem normal." Paul spoke out loud. The tv static crackling within the spans of silence, the pixelated graphics, and the 4 security guards surrounding Roman combines seemed…bizarre. This all seemed a little too serious, Paul just knew something was about to happen. Then Roman spoke, his voice was distorted and almost unrecognizable. "In 30 minutes it will all start, don't try to hide or run, everyone will eventually get caught, there's no point. I will hold you in my cells until I find a job for you. I will be nice though, everyone living with a family will get put in a cell next to one another. It's not like it's the end of the world, it's just the end of all your boring lives.

Working day in, day out with no real benefit to the world, you need to do something that will actually help our country." In the top right corner of the tv was a countdown: 12 minutes and 31 seconds. Paul sat in shock, he knew he had to help but what was he supposed to do against a trillion dollar company with the power of a corporate god. Paul was overwhelmed with thoughts of anger. After facing his own sense of denial, a shrieking sound came from the tv, the timer hitting zero.

A loud thud came from the door, then another, then another, growing louder and stronger until… a crack. The door ripped off its hinges and dropped heavily to the ground. Ten armed men stormed inside and Paul sprinted for cover, hiding behind his kitchen counter waiting for the perfect time to jump out the window of his room.

Ten men stood outside watching incase he left while the other ten searched for him inside. Paul needed a distraction, he grabbed a mug from his kitchen counter and threw it at the other side of the hall. When the crash of the cup hit, Paul dashed for the window, quickly opening it and jumping outside.

There was a massive hill that Paul landed on from his window and he immediately tucked into a roll and hurled down the hill at a rapid speed.

He continued to gain momentum until he crashed in a bush that stopped him cold. Getting up, Paul looked around, seeing flashlights radiating from his house and the crackling sounds of walkie talkies coming from the building. He knew he couldn't take on all 20 of the men so he made a mad dash for the nearest safe place he could find.

Paul didn't know where he was going but he knew he had to get as far away from them as he could and figure out a plan from a place of safety.

His legs started to cramp up and that's when he knew he had to stop. He sat down heavily at the foot of a tree and looked up at the sky. It was filled with flashing lights and the sounds of screams could be heard piercing the night. Paul closed his eyes and fell asleep, hoping this was all a dream.

Waking up from his rest Paul had momentary hope, hope for a way out of this mess. He slowly stood up, taking in his surroundings. The screaming had died down but everything still looked like a dump.

Paul brushed the dirt off himself and started walking in the direction he came from. It felt like he was walking for hours until he finally reached the hill he had fallen from. The men who raided his house seemed like they were gone so he carefully crept up the hill. Jumping through his window he saw the state of his house, everything was broken and destroyed.

All he cared about right now was his car keys, if they didn't take them he could get out of this place and drive. He didn't have the faintest idea where, just that he needed to get out.
As if guided by a miracle, Paul spotted his car keys resting on the kitchen counter. He dashed to grab his keys and hurried out of the house.

Once he unlocked his car door and landed in the front seat, he felt a wave of relief rush over him, a sense of hope and safety he had been hoping for that whole night. Paul turned on the engine of the car and sped off, not knowing where he would possibly stay. While Paul was driving he passed by multiple houses, run down by this attack.

Paul got mad, really mad, and without thinking he was on his way to a set destination: Las Vegas, home of K.R Enterprises, the company behind this attack.

Now, here we are, Paul in his car driving to Vegas to take down these gruesome attackers.

Paul has not rested or stopped driving since the start, fearful or what might happen if he does. Two miles away from Vegas, Paul prepares for the worst.

Driving through a town along the desolate desert road, he saw something. On a light post there was a paper, a bounty, with his face on it. The bounty was worth a million dollars.

This spiked Paul's heartbeat but he stayed calm, he now knew this would be much harder than he expected. Arriving on the outskirts of Las Vegas, Paul noticed the high security around the entire city. The air was filled with drones and hundreds of men guarded a secure gate around an extremely tall building in the far distance. Paul, after realizing the attention the car would draw, decided to park far away and proceed on foot.

Scattered on the ground were heaps of trash and debris that Paul dodged. One piece of stray "trash" piqued Paul's interest, a flyer with information regarding an event for all workers of *K.R Enterprises* that they must go to. The best part about this was noticing who was going to be there, none other than the owner, Roman Pond.

Instantly Paul knew exactly what to do, sneak into this event and get Roman to himself so he can force him to stop this attack.

Executing this plan would be next to impossible, but he had to try.

Paul quietly walked behind a stone wall so no one could see him.

The event was one day away. To get into it he'd need a proper disguise. Lucky for Paul, there were plenty of guards, unlucky for him there was nowhere he was safe. He just needed to wait for the perfect time to run out from behind the safety of the wall he was hiding behind and into an abandoned house.

Laying on the ground next to him was a glass bottle left from the debris. Paul picked it up and got ready to throw it. He hucked the bottle as far as he could so the guards would look the opposite way.

As the sound of glass shattering pierced the ears of all the guards around, they turned to look at the commotion, giving Paul the chance to make a mad dash for the nearest house.

He made it to the house, locking the door behind him. Having a place to rest made him think even more, and he wondered how exactly he was going to get a guard uniform?

He'd convinced himself he didn't need rest but the second he sat down on the couch for a break he fell fast asleep. Hours passed until he finally woke up from his slumber.

Paul jolted awake and realized what he had done, he had wasted precious time he needed for his disguise. Now with only five hours left he needed to speed it up.

Ideas rushed through his head but none seemed to click with him, until there, he found it, the perfect way to take a uniform.

Paul sped out the house, still silent, but gaining more speed in every step he took. He made his way around taking the alleyways to avoid being spotted. Finally, across the street Paul saw a gas station.

This was perfect for Paul's plan, he would act like his uniform went missing and somehow steal one from another guard. Paul hid his face with a hat he found in the alley and walked up to the gas station.

Shoving the door open Paul expected to encounter a normal civilian running the front desk, instead he saw a worker for K.R.

Paul walked up and politely asked, "Can you help me?"

"Ya, what do you need, boss?" replied the worker.

"I was just using the bathroom and left for a second to grab something and when I came back my uniform was gone." Paul convincingly spoke.

"Oh shoot! I can check the bathroom if you want me to just in case it's still in there."

"Would you actually do that?"

"Of course, man."

This was exactly what Paul was hoping for and saw his opportunity approaching. They both arrived at the bathroom and walked inside.

"I don't see anything man." The worker remarked.

"Can you just take a closer look, please?" Paul asked.

After saying this Paul pulled out the hidden sleeping spray in his side pocket and misted its contents all over the bathroom. Paul was able to cover his mouth and nose and get out but the other guy was caught in the fumes. While he was knocked out on the floor, it was a perfect time for Paul to steal his uniform. Paul snatched the workers uniform and ran right back to the house he had been staying in.

One hour to the event. Paul suited up and got ready for what was about to go down. He walked out of his house scared but ready to end this all. Paul walked past all the guards and straight to the large tower of K.R Enterprises. When he entered the building he was astonished, it was massive and beautiful.

After a minute of admiration Paul snapped out of it and focused back on the job at hand. The event was taking place in the ballroom on the third floor. Paul entered the elevator and rode it up.

When the doors opened he was greeted by thousands of people, all employees of Roman. Luckily, Paul blended in and was able to find a place out of the way where he could watch his arrival.

After twenty minutes of patiently waiting, he saw him being ushered in by ten guards, surrounded on all sides, immediately beelining to the room in the back. That was Paul's cue.

He quickly walked the same way to the door that Roman had just walked into. Two guards were blocking the door and he knew he couldn't get in that way. Making a split second decision, he ran to the bathroom.

On the walls of the bathroom was a vent, Paul looked out for any people potentially going to enter and when he saw no one approaching he unscrewed the vent and dove in.

Shimmying through the vents, Paul was very uncomfortable and dirty. Through the vents, Paul could hear Roman faintly talking, reciting his lines.

He crawled in the direction of the voice and reached the room. Looking down Paul, could see four guards and Roman. The room was a basic white room with mirrors and a large couch.

Creating a distraction would not be possible in this situation, he had to go the hard way. Paul unlatched the vent and dropped into the room. Everyone in the room was extremely startled and immediately went on the attack.

His training made it so that he was able to easily out maneuver all the guards with some fast movement and was able to tie them all up with a rope that he found on the ground. It was just him and his target now. Roman was sitting in the corner, extremely scared of what was going to happen to him.

Then Paul spoke, "Why would you do this? What is your purpose behind this? This is all too cruel."

"I want power, I want everyone to kneel before me, including you." Roman maliciously spoke.

"That's never going to happen, just give it up already. You're in a corner, literally."

"You forget I have all the power and not some wanna be ninja like you."

"At least I'm not the one that has to cower in a corner. This could all be over, just shut it all down, open the cells and let everyone free."

"And why would I do that? I would rather give my life up than have this whole operation go down. You know another person can just take over after me? I already set up this attack in all seven continents, what makes you think I am the end to this?"

"I will take this down and I will take you down"

"My life means nothing in this, this is the world takeover, a single person can't take down a worldwide attack."

"I will fight until the day I die and I will be known for that."

"And how will people know you if K.R controls the media? Your life will mean nothing, just give up."

"It didn't have to go like this Roman."

"I would never give in to you."

"Goodbye Roman."

The sword went right through, he was a hologram.

Judah Camille

Judah Camille is a student at WISH Academy High School who enjoys exploring the nature of fiction, mystery, and slowly unraveling each story, dissecting it piece by piece. She began writing when she had just transitioned into the 6th grade (2020), being stuck in the house gave her a plethora of things to write about. When not writing, Judah likes to sing and act. This is her first published story.

Unexpectedly
by Judah Camille

Unexpectedly, I feel the sudden urge to share my final thoughts. The time between this day and when my mother passed, I knew I wouldn't say anything.

Not even thinking, or controlling my body I stood. I stood like never before because this time,
I wasn't aware.

As I started stepping closer and closer to the podium I realized that I wasn't just taking thoughtless steps,

I stepped for my little siblings who would grow up never hearing their mother sing them to sleep again,

I stepped for my dad who had lost his first and only love after 20 years of partnership so unexpectedly,

I stepped for my Grandma who lost her only child, who cared for her dearly, I stepped for the friends which my mom made in this journey of life and all of their memories, I stepped for the teachers who had once congratulated her for many accomplishments, I stepped for the little girl in her, young Daniele Baumen who would never know that she would pass so unexpectedly.

I took my final step reaching the podium for the little girl in me who believed her mother would stay forever and sing her to sleep.

Reaching the podium was the hardest thing. As I looked over all of my friends and family, It seemed as If they were all submerged in my tears. I opened my mouth struggling to speak, but trying to profess my truth. I looked left and right over everyone looking for some form of support. Breathing heavily, I skimmed the room until I locked my eyes on a picture of Mom.

Inanimate, she still brought me peace, a gap in my heart was temporarily filled by seeing her beautiful smile once more. Trying to step towards the picture I'm unexpectedly stopped, My father is holding me back from seeing my mother for one final time.

He looked at me as if this gave him some sort of pleasure keeping me away. I push him off of myself in an attempt to escape, but not long before both of my younger siblings barricaded me, blocking me away from mom.

"AHHHHH," I screamed at the top of my lungs attempting to pass through. I tried, I tried with all my might to go through, but all of the sudden, it was as If they each had the strength of giants. "NO, NO, PLEASE" I cried as more family and friends blocked me from mom. I screamed, I screamed like never before crying for a lost connection to her which I had never felt before. This was the first time she wasn't here to protect me...

Unexpectedly. I hear a voice. Calming and familiar.
I try to look around but suddenly everything becomes dark.

"Shhhhh, calm down honey It's alright calm down. I'm with you." As I slowly become more aware I can feel the tears streaming down my face. The same calm, familiar voice . A sweet kiss lands on my forehead waking me up from my sleep. There's my mother soothing my bad dreams. In disbelief. I say nothing. I stared at her to analyze her features to assure myself that this is real. Noticing my odd behavior, she lays next to me and begins to sing. I can't control my emotions now due to the fact that my mother starts crying as she holds me close. " My baby" she says once her song is over. Both our faces resting, Finally, I feel at peace.

Tristan R.

Tristan R. is a WISH Academy High School student who enjoys stories like onions where you can learn and see something new with each viewing. He began writing after taking Ms. Avalos' English class, where she inspired me to tell my own stories. When not writing, Tristan R. likes to play sports and play games. This is his first published story.

Haiku
by Tristan

Ninety nine one goal
Score a goal to make it once more
Whole broken no more

Kristy Rodriguez

Kristy Rodriguez is a student at WISH Academy High School who enjoys cheesy romance books along with suspenseful thrillers. She began writing when she was 8, when she got inspired by several romance action movies. When not writing, Kristy likes to read, color, and watch movies. This is her first published story.

Why Her?
by Kristy Rodriguez

"Here I am to confirm that Lesie Beckham is dead." Officer James said with no expression on his face, as if he had no remorse for Lesie or her family. Everyone was silent. So silent you could've heard an ant eating. It was the town meeting that was hosted at the head church, every Friday at 6, here is where you would get all the newest gossip or news. Britney personally hated being there just because people would force information out of you but you had no choice. Today was different, no one was moving out of their chairs gossiping with one another.

After what felt like years passing by, officer James left off the stage leaving everyone there stunned. Britney's mom, Tessa, felt like she had no choice but to get up and leave. She couldn't stand being there another second. After Tessa left, it gave the rest of the crowd the opportunity to also leave. Britney got up and started heading to her moms car, even though Britney knows how to drive her mom still forces Britney to not drive around her. Britney noticed her mom was walking faster than normal, it was a bit unusual since her mom hated fast walkers. In the sunlight Tessa's hair was a golden Blonde making her hair stand out compared to everyone else. Britney tried to not think of it too much since her hair was different from both of her parents. She decided to walk towards the car and try to forget about the news she just heard inside the church.

The car ride home was awkward as Tessa was trying to make small talk, "So are you going to Tara's house when we get home?"

"Yea I'm picking up Chelsea and we are heading over to Tara's. Is it cool with you if I stay at her house tonight?" Britney was 18 years old and was still scared to ask her mom to go hangout at times.

"Yes, that's fine, can you just make sure to get home at 11 tomorrow?" Tessa looked scared like if she was unsure whether or not to let Britney go to Tara's house "Sure." She wasn't sure why but she didn't want to ask.

The rest of the car ride was silent as they were pulling up to the house. They both came out of the car, Britney went straight to her room to get her bag for the sleepover. She had already packed her bag the day before so she just got it and went straight back to her car now. She had promised Chelsea to be at her house by 1:30 and it was currently 1:12. Luckily Chelsea's house wasn't too far from her house.

After ten minutes she got to Chelsea's house and texted her saying she was there. Britney was still thinking about Leslie. How could someone do such a thing? Before she could think about what the police had said earlier, her door opened and Chealsea appeared.

"Hey, sorry for making you wait. I needed to use the restroom real quick before I came in." Chealsa looked so happy and so excited like nothing else mattered in the world.

¨Don't worry about it. You didn't take long. I was wondering if you wanted to stop by at the store for snacks before we head to Tara´s?¨

¨Yea sounds good I'm starving.¨ Chelsea said while rubbing her stomach, signaling she was hungry.

¨Cool I'm gonna go to the one close to Tara's house so she won't wonder why we are taking forever.¨

On the way to the store Chelsea and Britney were just talking about what had happened earlier in the day at the town meeting. Chelsea wasn't there but word spread quickly and everyone in the town already knew.

¨Who do you think did it? Chelsea asked if she looked scared as if she already knew who did it.

¨I have no idea but I don't think they live here. Who in their right mind would grow up here and still do that to someone, I'm convinced someone random person just came by town saw Leslie and did you know what.¨

This was the only thing that Britney could have done without scaring herself. Thinking about someone in town that did that to Leslie is still in the town. She might know them too and that's what terrified her the most.

¨Honestly you never know who it could be. For all we know it can be our old English teacher. He was mean anyways.¨

¨Yea he was but that doesn't mean he was the person who killed Leslie.¨

Britney tried to believe her own words but when she was really thinking about it, she couldn't put it past Mr. Lowvoski.

Britney pulled into the store's parking lot and both of them got down from the car, entering the store.

"Let's be quick so Tara doesn't think we ditched her." Chelsea said, trying to hurry out of the store.

Okay do you want to take some chips and drinks?" Britney asked Chelsea since she knew she was the most hungry.

"Yea and also can you get me a slice of pizza or do you just want to get a full pizza? Oh my god look." Chelsea nodded towards the man standing across from them, behind the counter. It was Charles.

Briney used to have the biggest crush on him ever. One day she was going to confess her feelings to time and then she saw he was with another girl already. She already knew she had no chance with him, he was the nicest man in the town and every girl had a crush on him, he would help with the town's meeting and would volunteer at every store to make sure they wouldn't be understaffed. If they were he would ask for him to be a part timer just for that day. On top of everything he did, girls also liked him because he was handsome. With his blonde hair, it wasn't too long but it also wasn't short. He was tall and had tattoos. Britney had seen him in the morning at the town meeting so it wasn't unusual to see him around the town.

"What? It's just Charles." Britney still hid that she had a crush on him but it wasn't a big one. She didn't even want to tell her friends.

"Yes it's Charles I'm not dumb but i was gonna ask did you see anything weird at the town meeting today? I was going to go but you know how I am when it comes to those meetings. They give me such a weird feeling." Chelsea was terrified of the town meetings.

"No?? What are you talking about just spill it." Chelsea was starting to scare Britney "Well it was said that the guy who, you know, was there at the town meeting and Charles knows who it is but instead of Charles telling the police he just started crying. Chelsea was telling the story like she was reading it off a book.

Britney did remember Charles crying but she thought it was because of Leslie, everyone in the town knew Charles treated Leslie like his own child.

"Chelsea you're being ridiculous he was crying because Leslie is dead." Right when she said those words she regretted it immediately. She had said it too loudly. Britney turned and went to the register trying to leave now.

"Why? Did you have to bring that up now?" Charles said while looking at Britney. His eyes didn't look sad but instead they just looked like they were full of hatred.

I know I´m sorry Charles I didn't mean it. It was just in the moment. I didn't mean to offen-" Before she could finish her sentence Charles threw back her chips in her face.

"WHY? WHY WOULD YOU HAVE TO BRING THAT UP? YOU HAVE NO IDEA WHAT YOUR TALKING ABOUT."

Charles started screaming at Britney, and when he started yelling, Chelsea began to slowly make her way towards both of them, worried but surprised.

"OKAY I'M SORRY I'M TELLING YOU I DIDN'T MEAN IT. STOP SCREAMING."

Britney was frightened. She had no idea why Charles started to act like this.

"Hey turn around."

Britney turned around thinking Chelsea was going to help her try to calm Charles down. Then all of a sudden she felt a harsh pain on her forehead.

Chelsea had hit Britney with her purse. Britney fell to the floor holding her head, not knowing what to do in this situation.

"What the heck was that for?" Britney couldn't even look up from the floor as her head was still hurting. She was so confused at the moment, not even processing in her brain what was happening.

"Isn't it obvious? Gosh, you really don't pay attention to anyone but yourself don't you?" Chelsea asked as she pushed Britney's head more, making her hurt even more.

"Don't even waste your time with her, it's not worth it." Charles said as he was making his way around the counter getting closer to both of the girls.

As Charles was getting closer, Britney was trying to look for a way out with the one eye she had opened, the other eye closed since she was holding it shut while also holding her head. In the corner of her eye she could see a small figure coming towards the door.

She tried to get a closer look so she could call for help. Unless it was someone working with Charles and Chelsea. Slowly and slowly she got closer to the door and lifted her head just the slightest. Just enough so she could see outside but not enough so Chelsea and Charles could see. She could try to get out by the door, but the bell ringing would have been a dead getaway. So she decided to get help from outside the window.

Before she was looking outside she turned around to make sure they wouldn't notice. They both were whispering to each other, maybe figuring out what they were going to do next.

She found this as a perfect opportunity for her to try to call for help. She very quietly and leisurely looked out of the window. When she looked outside she still saw the small figure but now it was a bit bigger as it was getting closer. Now, she could actually see who the person was. It was Mr. Lowvosqi.

Britney hoped on everything he wasn't with Charles and Chelsea, and he would actually be able to help her. She didn't know if he was or not so all she could do was wave her hand to her teacher. She tried not to do it too high but also she wanted him to notice her. He saw her hand. Mr. Lowvosqi looked confused, like he didn't know if she was joking or not.

"What's wrong?" His lips read.

"Help me!" Instead of her lip saying it, she accidentally said it out loud. Both Charles and Chelsea looked up at Britney noticing she was all the way towards the window. Chelsea stopped talking to Charles and went right beside Britney. Chelsea looked out the window and saw Mr. Lowvosqi. She just smiled and waved at him as if she wasn't doing anything wrong.

That's when Mr. Lowvosqi stopped and turned around, making his way back to his car. "No please Mr. " Britney started yelling but he couldn't hear it. He was already on his phone inside his car.

" Yea now you don't have any help do you Britney?" Chelsea was taunting Britney, making fun of her. Chelsea kicked her head again where it had already hurt.

"I just don't understand why you're doing this." Britney said to both of them looking back and forth now crying.

"Oh wow acting all innocent now. Let me tell you the reason." Chelsea was now bending down towards Britney.

"Long long ago, during our freshman year when we had the movie competition and we all had to create a 5 minute movie. You partnered up with Leslie and in the movie there is a small clip, probably like 6 seconds long. In the background you see me. I'm in the background and I'm with James. Do you know where I'm going with this?" Chelsea said, looking at Britney with pure hatred in her eyes.

"You're mad because you didn't like the way you looked in the video? That's what this is about?" Britney was trying to think of every possible scenario, trying to figure out what she did wrong.

"No. Gosh in the video I'm with James and we were right next to each other, during that time i was with Ken. He didn't want me and James to even be near each other but you and Leslie caught me and him on footage and he broke up with me. He broke up with me. I loved him Britney you don't know and I lost him and it's all because of you. Chelsea felt so angry all she could do in that moment was to push Britney down again.

Right when she pushed her the bell jingled and the door opened. The cops were there. All three of them froze. When three cops entered so had Mr. Lowvosqi. He called the cops and he came to help Britney.

"Put your hands where I can see them now, both of you." Officer James had ordered looking at Chelsea and Charles. One cop was with Charles who was standing next to Chelsea while she was talking to Britney. They both put their hands up.

Both cops had got their hands and put them in handcuffs. They took them outside where they was three cop cars and Mr. Lowvosqi´s car where it was earlier. Turns out he had never left; he stayed in his car, called the cops, and waited for them to arrive. Another cop went next to Britney made sure she was okay. That cop had taken Britney out to the Police car just to examine her more clearly.

While the cop was looking at her she could see Chelsea leaving in the cop car, she was looking out the window. Chelsea had spotted Britney and Chelsea's face had turned into a smirk. "Were you friends with her?" The cop asked Britney.

"No." Britney was thinking, all those fun times she had with Tara and Chelsea. They were all a lie.

Britney had remembered the sleepover with Tara and decided to call her. The phone was ringing and she was waiting, thinking about whether or not Tara knew about Chelsea. After a couple of seconds Tara's voice was now on the phone.

"Hey I've been waiting for you guys where are you?" Tara wasn't at the store while Chelsea and Charles were in the store and she sounds seriously concerned. So maybe she didn't know about Chelsea.

"Hey I'm gonna head over there soon. We have a lot to talk about." Britney was telling Tara as she walked to her car, heading to Tara's house.

"Oh what's up?"

"It's about Chelsea."

"What about her?"

More like why her?

Ryan Scott

Ryan Scott is a student at WISH Academy High School who enjoys writing about the human experience. He began writing back when he was very young, inspired by the many books he read. When not writing, Ryan likes to bake, read, and hang out with his pet cat Piper. This is his first published story.

How to Make It Perfectly
by Ryan Scott

INGREDIENTS:
- 1 of that thing
- 3 of the other
- A pinch of this
- ½ of another
- ¾ of that at first, another ⅔ for later
- Just a dash of it for a final touch

STEPS:

1. Make sure to prepare everything before beginning! First, set this up properly so that the finished product doesn't get stuck.
2. Mix together that thing with the other thing. Make sure you mix it at the perfect speed, as it won't work if you don't.
3. Set that aside and go to this place. At the right setting, combine the first ¾ of that with another. Wait a bit, making sure that it doesn't get messed up. Add a pinch of this.
4. Fold together some of the first with some of the second. Make sure it's in the right proportions! Don't overfold it, but make sure it's folded perfectly. Repeat with the rest of the first and then the rest of the second.
5. Now is when you bring back what you set up. Layer the extra ⅔ of that, then put the rest on top. Now wait for it to finish!
6. Once you know it's finished, add a dash of it on top for a final touch, and voilà! I don't respond to emails for help, but the recipe will guide you better than I can anyway. Enjoy it!

RATE THIS RECIPE: ☆☆☆☆☆

Socaia T. ★★★★★

1/1/25 Thanks for the amazing recipe! I'll be sure to share it with all of my friends ☺

Adrienne Sworde

Adrienne Sworde is a student at WISH Academy High School who enjoys writing short poems. She began writing at a very young age. When not writing, Adrienne likes to paint. This is her first published story.

Oak Trees Only Grow Outside
by Kristy Rodriguez

In my quiet home, there is a loud metallic rattle.
As the Gardener unlocks my door, the keys and padlocks battle.
The decaying wood of my floor creaks and shouts and yells,
throwing up a cloud of dusts and dirts and things that smell.

My scales, still just withered and dry,
suddenly crumble happily
knowing that it is time.

She creeps in, moving twice to the left and then once right,
For the floor of this old basement has tricks and traps that bite.
She steps quite closer and the metal that confines me reflects
upon her face.
"I'm so lonely, talk to me, please Gardener," I scream silently
from my cage.

And then it happens, a drink of life,
within these rotting walls,
I've found that I'm again revived.

"My precious acorn, small and weak,
You're safest in here, close to me.
When you grown into a big strong Oak,
I might finally have to let you go,
But for now it seems that this old cage,
Is where you'll have to stay."

But as long as the acorn breathes in the basement mold,
Her entire life will be controlled.
The story of the Oak will never begin
and the lonely acorn can never win.
For the acorns who stays in their dark, cold rooms,
will never know what it is like to bloom.

Abby Obregon

Abby Obregon is a student at WISH Academy High School who enjoys world building, creating characters, connecting fantasy stories to real life situations, and writing and reading fantasy stories. She began writing around the time of Covid where she could get lost in her own worlds away from reality and express emotions and wants she couldn't before. When not writing, Abby Obregon likes to draw, watch dystopian movies and shows and spend time with her family. This is her first published story of hopefully many more to come.

Kiko's Story
by Abby Obregon

There once was a time when all the nations lived together in harmony; at least, that's what the elders say. The first Goddess awoke in an empty world between space and created life itself, but she also wanted to share her creation with beings like her. With the fire within her heart, she created Aurush, and with light, there needed to be dark, so she created Hala. She created Arno with the flow of water from her hair mixed with the soil from the ground to help create and control life in the land, and finally, Rayyan from her own breath from her lungs to help cultivate the land. Nobody really knows who came first, if those were really names of the gods, or even if the first Goddess existed at all, but at some point in their existence, they all decided to create beings themselves. Primarians, we are called, born from the hands of the gods. They granted their powers to us, their children holding the power of fire or the power of their land. When they thought it was time, they left the land to the Primarians, to continue to live and strive together in harmony. What they didn't know was that it would create a dispute.

The Halans decided they were superior, teaming up with the Aurushians to conquer and claim their own land and soon reigning hell on the other Primarians of Arnos and Rayyans. The primarians moved to their own land, forming nations and separating from each other. For centuries, they were at war. The discovery of portals or possibly the boredom of the fire and dark nations finally brought the wars to a close, and several parts of the nations were in poverty.

I live in a small unnamed village in the forests of Arno. My dad's father was a warrior in the war, and he himself barely missed the war, somehow he met my mom, and they had me along with my younger siblings. Like in every world in every universe, there were terms of currency, bills, and coins. Similar to that we had crystals, gems, and minerals that all had certain value to buy materials to make a house or keep your way out of starvation. My family had very little of it. I was walking down the cobblestone lined roads, the chilly morning a reminder of the sheer and tattered clothes I wore that were kept together with rope and other animal hides. I was to shop for the week's food.

"Just one husktorn fish please."

I gave the seller the pressed crystals that my father had given me for the food. Looking around the roads of the bustling market square was a reminder to the diversity of my home town. The market square was the only part of town where everyone got together and coexisted peacefully. Every seller had their stalls open here where every Primarian was welcomed to buy, even the huge trolls that resided in the woods came out once in a while to take a gander.

"Kiko? Is that you girl?" A soft yet scratchy voice called my name. I knew who it was before I turned to look at her. Blair. Her skin was tanned from the sun and her hair a silky long black. Contradictory to my own hair with my ginger strands chopped to a short bob.

"You look so different. Your hair looks cute." She complimented me.

I hadn't seen her since she had dropped out of school, I had dropped out not soon afterwards. Since then, I had cut my long hair to be some to put more food on the table, not that I would tell her that.

"Oh.. yeah thank you," I smiled. "You look good yourself." I told her as I pointed out the clothes on her body that definitely kept her warm.

"Yeah! Thanks. Work has been high since the trade between the water villages down the mountain begun."

I knew what "work" she referred to. Mugging from the travelers hoping to trade or even just explore the world up here.

"Yeah." I simply mumbled.

I wrapped my arms around myself, suddenly self conscious of the clothing I had to keep together so I wouldn't have to worry about my parents spending money on extra clothes for me. She seemed to notice because she just smiled and rested her rough hand against my shoulder.

"You know…" She started before she looked around before back to me. "I'm actually a man short for this next coming up job. I'm in need of a lookout. Later tonight when the fisherman come back up with their carts, we're taking they're loot but there's also word of guards around from the palace. It's high pay."

I looked around, fiddling with my bag as if I was afraid someone would hear her giving me this offer.

"I- uh I don't know Blair."

"Come on. It's high pay, and you're off to the side anyway. No one will see you."

She stared at me for a moment, as if trying to figure out what was going on through my mind. I didn't even know what was running through my head. No matter how low crystals were in my family, my parents always taught me to never steal. If I got involved in that work now…

"Well… think about it. Tonight by the passage not far from the entrance of the village." She told me. She patted my shoulder before smiling and began walking off. Leaving me to my thoughts.

"Uh. Excuse me.. little girl. Your fish." The voice of the seller knocked me out of my thoughts.

"Oh! Sorry! Thank you."

Later that night I found myself laying in my bed sizes way too small for my body to lay flat down on its rickety surface. I stared at a painting of me and my friend Sienna. Even if she had a different situation from mine, she was like family to me. A sister I could rely on. I knew she wouldn't approve of the situation that I was about to go through. But I needed to. For my family. I looked towards the bed my little sister and brother shared, huddled together with the blanket only covering one of them. I knew what I needed to do.

Walking in the night, even when I tried my best to keep my footsteps quiet, they seemed louder than ever, matching the thumping of my heart against my chest. I never had snuck out before, at least not in the nighttime where the village seemed to be a ghost town.

Not too long after the cobblestone beneath my feet began to

transition into dirt and gravel. My feet seemed to be louder with the crunch beneath my feet. My mind was just as loud telling me to turn back but, I was already a long walk away.

"Kiko!" A hushed whisper called me from within the trees.

I quickly turned my body, tense in fear from who could be calling me. But it revealed Blair, hiding in the dark with a black cloak.

"Glad you could make it." She smiled as she reached out and pulled me into the darkness. We hid behind the trees in a small clearing full of people that looked older than us. Though with a wave of Blair's hand they moved away in which I could assume into their positions. Blair and I seemed to be the youngest and yet Blair was in charge.

"Alright. We've got to do this quickly. There's a tree not far down the path marked with a swirl symbol. Climb it and hide in the leaves when you see the wagon blow this whistle once. Well handle the rest." She instructed me.

I nodded my head, my body moving before my head could even process what was going on.

"What do I do if the guards come?"

"Blow it twice."

With that she tossed the hood over her head and disappeared into the dark. I followed her instruction and wandered down the path, finding an engraving of a swirl just as she had instructed and quickly climbed the tree.

Now all I had to do was sit quietly and wait to see a wagon travel up the path. The anticipation was killing me, the cold night air harsh against the sweat in my forehead.

Then, a rickety sound of wheels began running up the path. The wagon was here! I brought the small wooden whistle to my lips, a low whistle sound escaped out the other end, sounding almost like an owl.

The wagon passed by me and all I could do was watch as I pressed myself against the log of the tree. It went far enough that it was almost too deep in the dark to make out any details, and I almost thought that I had ruined the job. But as quickly as the wagon came it came to a stop, and suddenly I heard silent cries of struggling men.

Luckily I couldn't see anything. I tried not to think of the Primarians in the wagon, being robbed of the things they worked hard for in the dark. They probably couldn't even see the ones taking from them.. beating them. It suddenly went quiet… too quiet. It reminded me of my job to look out for oncoming guards. I glanced around the trees, too dark and no sign of more wagons or the thumping feet of guards. I heard a knock from below me causing me to quickly look down. It was Blair smirking up at me, she always seemed to catch me off guard. Maybe from practice of keeping her feet quiet in jobs like these. She must've been doing this her whole life, seeing as her father had done the same before.

"Get down here. Jobs done." She ordered.

Slowly I climbed down, finding my way through the trees wasn't unfamiliar to me. Growing in a village surrounded by the woods required learning how to travel through the natural landscape.

It's something we valued as Arno's. The natural world gifted by the gods.

"Good job." She said with a low chuckle.

She tied a string around the whistle before tossing it over my neck.

"Expect pay tomorrow morning. You're done here. My crew and I will do the dirty work."

I simply nodded my head, staying quiet. My hand went up the whistle around my neck as she gave me a pat on the back and bang to wander back to the now fallen wagon. My gaze landed on what I could only assume was who used to be the driver of the wagon, now laying on the ground. I woke up in my bed, getting up to stretch out my body that had to be curled up to fit in my bed. My siblings were out of bed already, I could hear their chatter outside the small room we shared. "Kiko!! Someone left a package for you. I've gotta go to work. Love you!" Shouts of my busy mom who left with a slam of the door.

I walked out, patting my little brother on the head before finding the envelope on the table. It was thick, I felt a heaviness fill my chest in a reminder of what I had aided in last night.

"What's that what's that!" My little brother asked as he jumped in the creaky wooden chair.

"Nothing Axel," I mumbled. "Hurry up and get to school with your other sister." I tried to offer him a smile. He brought another scoop of porridge to his mouth before tossing a bag over his shoulders and running out where Priscella waited for him. Fortunately they still had the option of school.

After I ensured they were away from the small house I ripped apart the paper of the envelope, stacks of pressed crystals falling onto the table. I froze. It was about one of my parents' full months of pay.

Knock knock knock!

I quickly turned to the door piling some papers and books onto the gems. I walked over to the door, I'm surprised that it still hadn't fallen down now. I slowly opened it but quickly busted in a person that wrapped their arms around me.

"Kiko! Hi!" She said excitedly.

Sienna. My best friend.

"Oh hi!" I smiled as my arms instinctively wrapped back around her.

"I just wanted to stop by before I went to school."

I smiled but I didn't know what to say as we pulled away. It only reminded me more of how different we were. She was one of the only people that had tried to get me to stay in school. Not even the teachers had bothered.

Her face carried the same warm smile it usually did but it quickly fell, along with her eyes to what was around my neck.

"Kiko..? What is.." She mumbled.

My fingers wrapped around the whistle before I even processed what she was looking at.

"Is that the Auron symbol!?"

Her hand immediately slapped my fingers away from my hand wrapped around the whistle. Her fingers around it before I could stop her. The Auron symbol she was referring to was the swirl of Blair's group. Auron.

"No- it's just- Blair gave it to me." I stammered.

"What!?"

As if she knew her eyes fell to the table behind me, I knew she could see the glint of the many crystals that littered the table.

"Kiko.." She sighed.

She pulled away, and the disappointment in her face filled the fuel of the disappointment I felt in myself. But for some reason as I glanced back at the table, the disappointment washed away. I had to do what needed to be done for my family right?

"I was just a lookout. I wasn't involved in anything major." I told her.

"Kiko. That's the same thing as being involved. Now you're a look out but what happens when you start leveling up?"

I knew she was right. Deep down I knew she was. But my family needed it. I could feel my hands clenching and unclenching at my sides, a sign of my nervousness.

"Sienna- it was just a one time thing. I swear." I said quietly.

Sienna just nodded her head slowly. Her hands just tightened around her school bag. She looked at the crystals before coming back to me.

"I've got to be going. There's other ways to get crystals, you know?" She told me.

I nodded my head back to her.

"Just- be safe."

As soon as she closed the door behind her I let out a soft sigh. My hand went to the whistle and I tucked it behind my shirt before I looked back to the table. I walked towards it and picked up the envelope, noticing there were even more crystals inside of it. There seemed to be some writing against the interior paper of the envelope. It read a time and a spot. Possibly a next mission. Question was, should I go back?

Over the next week I had more crystals than my family probably ever had. I surprised my siblings with random little gifts, more clothes and more food for the house. I even gave myself warmer clothes. It was the most we had in a long time. I was only the lookout for all the missions, never really having to come face to face with the people being mugged. It made me feel better, but that was probably stupid, I was a bystander in it after all, a helper. Though that didn't last really long.

"Oh come on Kiko. You've been doing good as a look out, sure but, you have the potential to make more girl." Blair chuckled. She nudged me with her shoulder a bit. I simply laughed and shrugged my shoulders. There had been many late nights, and I could feel the toll on my body. I don't know if I could handle being the one dealing with the people.

"I- I think I'm fine with the position I am in now you know?" I replied.

"Girl." She said with a look.

She threw her arm around my shoulder as we continued to walk. For a second I looked away from her, I spotted Sienna. A pit fell in my stomach. I waved slightly, Sienna just slightly smiled, she looked uncomfortable. Blair must've noticed this reaction because she pulled me closer.

"Hey. Look. If you don't start moving up I'm gonna have to kick you out the team man. It's just business." She warned. Her touch around my shoulder became uncomfortably tight. I didn't want to know what she meant by kicking me out of the team.

"O-okay. Alright. Yeah. Why not?" I smiled at her.

"That's the spirit! Look, we need you as soon as tonight. Got it? Be prepared to fight." I nodded a yes but looked back to see if I could spot Sienna. She was long gone by now.

"Okay. Get ready guys. Wagon will be here any minute." Blair was giving out orders since we arrived here.

Sitting down in the bushes, covered away with not only leaves but also the darkness of the night made me want to puke. I knew in just a few minutes that I would have to jump out of my cover and raid a wagon of unknown people, just to get some extra crystals in my pocket. Yet as I held the rope and axe tightly against my chest this sense of determination ran over my anxiety. I was already too deep in this.

"Let's go! Move!" A hushed voice ushered us forwards.

I could hear the familiar sound of wheels running along the crunchy gravel, the same noise I've heard several nights before.

I seemed to zone out in the moment which wasn't exactly something I had the luxury of doing often. But as I moved closer to the now stopped wagon I couldn't help but have these memories flash through my head, and I wasn't in the moment.

One second I finally made it out of the leaves and the next I'm standing next to the wagon. Sienna's voice ran through my head. *"Now you're a look out but what happens when you start leveling up?"*

I opened the wagon door and stood to the side as one of the bigger men dragged out a Primarian, she landed on the floor with a sharp thud.

"There's other ways to get crystals, you know?"

Someone stepped out of the wagon and instinctively I raised the blunt end of the axe to the side of their head, they fell with a dump to the ground. It seemed someone else had made it out of the wagon when I was knocking out the other and before I could react a sharp cold sliced over my eye which quickly burned warm. I cried out in pain and fell to the ground.

Before the man could do me any more damage he was brought down by someone else in the group, causing a bloodied knife to fall to the ground. I brought my hand to my eye, feeling the warm gooey liquid run over my palm and fill the crevices of the creases.

"Kiko!?" A stern voice snapped me out of it.

"On your feet. Get moving."

I stood up, remembering I had a job to do. I wrapped the rope given to me around another primarian, tying it with a knot I knew by heart. I couldn't see from the eye that had been slashed, and I could feel the thick liquid fall down my cheek like sweat. As soon as that was done I ran inside the wagon, taking anything valuable, anything that could be sold.

First night on this position of work and I already had a scar as proof of it. Yet I knew this wouldn't be my last night, even with this new gained scar. Not as long as I kept gaining my earnings.

"Where did that come from!?" It was Sienna, yelling over me… again.

"It's nothing Sienna. Just a scratch I got from a stick." At least that's what I had told my mom. I pushed her hand away and walked past her. I didn't want to think of the makeshift eyepatch I had over my eye to protect my wound and stop it from bleeding.

"A scratch from a stick doesn't wound you like that," She began chasing behind me. "You're still working for Blair aren't you?"

I ignored her calls. Every time we got together she would blabber about my life… my choices. She had even presented me with this new job position down the ocean by the water tribes. A steady source of income, and not putting my life in danger. A small shop opening up in need of a full group of members to work it. She claimed it would be better for me, for my future life. Now I had this scar for her to use against me that this was a dangerous line of work. But it got the money in, and it got it in quick. I was too deep in it anyway. I noticed I had been actively avoiding Sienna. Her, my mom, even my siblings in hopes of keeping my secrets hidden. Blair had been needing me more on jobs as well, away from keeping hidden in the dark for wagons to show up. No. Different jobs that required me to carry around our loot to sell to buyers, or hanging with groups of people to gain them as allies. And now with this scar as proof of my "loyalty" I had met quite a few new and different Primarians.

"What about it Sienna?" I said back.

I needed to meet up with Blair in a bit, but also I wanted to stop by the marketplace before I left, just to get a quick snack, a luxury I didn't have before.

"W-what about it!? I told you it was dangerous. I don't even see you anymore. You ignore my letters, and promise you're going to come by to see me but you never do." Sienna complained.

I stopped before finally turning to face her wide blue eyes.

"Sienna. I'm sorry. I really am. But I'm busy and I can't deal with your nagging right now." I said. She stopped and furrowed her eyebrows as if appalled from what I had just told her.

"*Nagging*? I'm not nagging you about anything! I'm worrying about you Kiko!"

"Not nagging? It sure feels like it. I can't talk to you without you bringing up what I do at least *once*."

"Is that why you've been avoiding me? Because you're afraid to hear the truth? I only bring it up because it's dangerous and I care for you Kiko. You're my best friend, of course I'm going to worry about you!"

I rolled my eyes and looked away from her. If she was part of one of the groups that I worked with I would've punched her square in the face.

"Stop worrying then Sienna. I don't need you to anymore. Blair was there for me and she's been there for me."

"Blair?? The only thing she's done as looking after you is offer you the job, and not even then was she looking out for you! She just needed somebody expendable."

"That's not true. You're only saying that because you're jealous." The words escaped me before I could even think.

She took a step back, her face contorted in a look that was almost disgust at my words. I was going to say something, anything to help my situation but my lips shut tight, standing my ground.

"Jealous? That's what you really think it is huh?" She said quietly. She sighed and ran a hand though her soft dirty blonde hair. "Well. You know what Kiko? That's it. That's it! I have had enough of this. I'm not going to bother anymore. You still have the option to leave and come over to the shop opening. But I guess it's your life. You decide what to do with it. This will be the final time I try to help you."

And with that she turned around to walk away.

I opened my mouth yet again, tempted to yell after her to fix my ego back in its place. I didn't know how to feel at that moment, not while I stood with my hands clenching at my sides as I watched my best friend walk away. What was there to feel when she claimed this to be the last time she tried to help me?

"Hey, Kiko. You seem kinda distracted there girl." Blair nudged me on the shoulder, it was sore from a job just the day before.

"Yeah. Yeah. Just thinking." I mumbled.

"Don't be getting cold feet on me now." She warned.

I had a feeling she didn't quite mean it in a friendly way. I just nodded and continued walking beside her. My hands continued to clench onto the bag slung over my shoulder, carrying ingredients for a certain potion that had been in high demand. We were to sell it to one of our buyers. Though she seemed to be an important customer, as Blair had to come with me. Fortunately Blair didn't push me on, most likely because she didn't even care. She just didn't want me to quit on her.

Blair had me wait away from her and the buyer, probably some words they had to exchange about business that I wasn't in a higher position to hear about yet. So I stayed put and looked around. We were by an old run down house, taken over by the elements of the forest. There seemed to be a shadow looming in every corner; there was not one Primarian in sight.

"Hey." A shout called me over to the next of them and I followed over to them.

I nodded to the buyer, she was an older woman. She tattoos all over her face and what I could see of her chest, signs of beauty and her story, just like how hair did. She had her own hair buzzed short, sign of either crimes she committed, losses, or a huge change in life. And judging by the scars on her pale skin that began to wrinkle, it was most likely the first option.

I slowly raised the bag towards her not before unclipping the opening though. She peeked inside and looked to one of her own people who stood still behind her. He was equally as scarred but had more hair on his head.

"This was less than what I had ordered." Her rough voice sternly informed us.

I quickly glanced over to Blair, she hadn't informed me on the low stock of supplies we were providing her with.

"I told you. You'd get a taste now and the rest once I ensure you're not a talker." Blair said. This seemed to piss off the lady.

Before any other words could be exchanged someone had gripped my neck and pulled me so I stumbled over my own footing. The lady now had me against her chest, her large hand around my neck and a sword to my back. I couldn't say anything with the force around my neck, my eyes widened as I looked to Blair for help, but she seemed calm as if she was out buying tea for dinner.

"I want what I paid for now. Or your worker here is done for." She warned, I could feel her hot breath behind me on the freckled skin of the back of my neck.

Blair merely smirked and tilted her head to the side as if testing the lady. "You think that's a threat? You don't think it's easy for me to find someone else for her spot?"

My eyes widened. I could feel a shiver run down my spine, my fingers instinctively raised to those of the ladies that curled around my neck. The lady just tightened her grip at Blair's words.

"Blair.." I managed to choke out.

Blair kept her cool.

I couldn't see it but I heard a sound of a single footstep behind me and the lady. I could imagine her worker patting her on the shoulder or just moving to remind her he was still there. She let go of me with a shove and I stumbled once more, Blair only just caught me.

"If I don't get the rest by tomorrow then I'll be talking." The lady spat out. She made a simple gesture to her buddy behind her and they turned to make their leave.

"Blair- what the- what happened back there." I coughed out.

"What?"

"What do you- I could've gotten killed."

"This entire job could get you killed, Kiko. Geez- relax yeah? It wasn't like she was actually gonna do it."

"She had the sword right against my back *Blair.*"

Blair rolled her eyes, her hand came up to my back right where the sword had been once pressed. She guided me away from the spot back where the hustle of Primarians began to be heard again.

"Look. I'll need you to drop off tomorrow alright? Make sure to bring a weapon in case." She warned me.

"She's twice my size, we know what happened last time I faced a person like that." I mumbled as I gestured to my eye covered in its patch.

"Sure but, if she ever gets you in a grip like that again, just go for the stomach. Got it?" She told me.

I just rolled my eyes and nodded my head once more. She patted me on the head with a chuckle as we continued to walk, on to the next job.

It had been a week or so of jobs like these and our usual thefts. I had managed to get the hang of things. With more food on the table and nicer things in the house the jobs were a simple blur, a necessity to make my home better. The more jobs I went on, the more distant I became with the people in my life that I already had been distant with. It didn't help that I no longer had my best friend by my side, my sister by soul not next to me anymore. Sienna. The bruises from the jobs just piled on, and I may have had to inflict some on other primarians as well. I was sore and tired everyday, despite it being something so common in my day to day life… I was at my lowest. Sienna has warned me plenty of times that I would get too deep into this life, and I have. She warned me it was dangerous, and it was. I knew it was. Yet it was still my decision to stay, my choice to dwell deeper.

My mother had asked me about all the extra crystals and extra food, but my father was too busy working than actually noticing the small details at home. I had lied to her, saying I had helped with the buyers at the market or extra change from Sienna. Though I think deep down she knew it wasn't luck that all of this was being brought home. She just didn't want to say anything. That was her choice. I guess even with support anyhow I would still work with Blair. Right? Crystals for home, for my roof, food and back. And the bodies of my family. Even with Sienna's support it was my choice to stay here.

"Blair." I said sternly.

She quickly turned to look at me, she looked surprised to see me.

"Hey girl. What's up? Jobs not yet for another hour." She said.

"I'm done." I quickly said. My eyepatch was off now, a scar that started from my eyebrow over my eyelid and down right above my cheek. The scar a sign of the hard work I had put in this.

"Wh-what? Why do you mean done?" She scoffed.

"I'm done. I want out."

She laughed at my face, her long braid that fell down to her waist swaying with her chuckle. Though I stayed quiet, I don't know why she was laughing. I finally mustered the courage to talk to her face to face about me not working for any longer. She quieted down and once she realized I was serious, her smile slowly died down.

"Out? You don't just get out of this type of business." She told me. Her arms crossed above her chest, she straightened up as if trying to appear more intimidating to me. I straightened up as well, she was definitely taller than me but I didn't feel the least bit irritated. Not anymore.

"I do. And I will." I muttered. I stepped closer to her, trying to see if she would make any moves of actually stopping me, she just scoffed.

"Yeah. Good luck with that girlie. Just see what happens

without my protection or my currency." Blair threatened me. My fingers clenched at my side, irritation and frustration pooling inside me like the blood that swirled in my veins.

"I don't need you." I whispered to her face. She didn't seem bothered, at least not outwardly but, I could see the anger and the annoyance swirling in her black orbs. She sucked in her cheek, as if biting back from shouting at my face. I knew it wouldn't be this easy. It couldn't be. I would have to face the consequences later, but for now, I was free.

I walked down the road, walking side by side with wagons I once aided in stealing from. I stayed silent and away from the chatter of the people walking down to the ocean side. It was my choice to quit and now my choice to be walking down and away from my home. Everyone seemed to be so happy, and carefree.

"Kiko?" Someone softly called out my name. I slowly turned around. Sienna was standing on the dock, just in front of the shop that was having its grand opening today. People lined the wooden flooring, excited at the new opportunities presented.

"Hey.." I said quietly.

"You made it." She said, a slight smile made it to her lips. Her eyes scanned my scar before focusing on just me once more. I looked down to my hands, suddenly feeling nervous.

"I quit." I muttered. Slowly I looked back up to her. Her expression seemed puzzled, almost hesitant to my words. "I'll figure out the rest of it once I return home. But I don't want to live that life anymore. I want to go down the right path, the best path for me and my family." I said softly, as if I was afraid to startle her.

She slowly nodded her head, a smile slowly forming on her lips.

"Yeah?" She let out a soft giggle. She slowly stepped forward and wrapped her arms around me, and my arms immediately wrapped back around her. "That's good… that's really good." She let out a chuckle, almost relieved to hear my words. I chuckled slightly back feeling a heaviness from my chest lift at her words in response to mine.

"Yeah." I whispered as I nodded my head. She pulled away from hugging me and stared at my face as if she was finally seeing me for the first time again.

"Come on. We got our new positions to find." She smiled. She grabbed my hand and led me to the store. It was covered in banners and lanterns lit by fireflies. The small store was bright and big in the way it brought opportunity for our communities to get together in one. There was going to be a lot of work ahead of me. But in the end it would be worth it. In the end this was the path I was meant to take. The safer path that would support me and my family, probably less than a more dangerous job. But safe. With my best friend beside me and a bright future ahead.

Adetoni Adewunmi

Adetoni Adewunmi is a student at WISH Academy High School who enjoys writing poems. She began writing in 7th grade when her teacher gave her a poetry assignment. When not writing, Adetoni likes to play games with her little brother and watch tv shows/ movies . This is her first published story.

Timed Dreams
by Adetoni Adewunmi

I have wrapped my dreams in a silk cloth,
Dreams are a special thing to you;
Dreams that wait for you when the time is right,
Stored in a box when things get tight

I have wrapped my dreams in a silk cloth;
Hidden in the gold box surrounded by the other bland boxes;
Hidden from society; hidden from the hatred

Dreams get faded over time, from the time you wasted;
New dreams get created, once faded

A silk cloth
Wrapped around dreams in a gold box;

The golden box still remains untouched, but carries dreams that
time has brushed.

Autumn

Autumn is a student at WISH Academy High School who enjoys reading realistic fiction stories. She began writing in elementary school and gained more talent for it in middle school. When not writing, Autumn likes to craft, have fun with her friends, or just relax. This is her second published story.

An Original Poem
by Autumn

Do they see me as more than an object on a shelf?

Are they unaware of the knowledge I carry?

There's a million of me, yet each has its own story

Each book is stacked with pages of thoughts, wonders, anticipation

Some have thicker more firm covers

Others have thin, loose veils

A trivial difference at first, until you flip the pages

Some books are noticed once, then left untouched

Layers of introspection, fascination, and suspense yet to be revealed

Why do they ignore some and take interest in others? Sure, a few are older or less conspicuous

But why should that change someone's motivation to look
deeper?
There's a million of us, yet each has its own story
And I'm sure they have theirs too

Daniil Humeniuk
Podborskyi

Daniil Humeniuk Podborskyi is a student at WISH Academy High School who enjoys writing fantasy and adventure stories. I started writing after taking My my inspired me to write and start telling my own story. When not writing, Daniil Humeniuk Podborskyi likes to play volleyball. This is his first published story.

Tales of a Wandering Flame
by Daniil H. Podborskyi

The Leaving of Middlemere

My name is Danrik, and I once thought magic was easy.

At Middlemere Academy, I studied under Lady Phamira, who made potion lessons feel like storytelling, and Sir Randor, who taught history like it was a living thing. We laughed, we dueled with light spells, we rode practice brooms that barely got off the ground.

But the day I received my letter from Ninth Realm High, everything changed. The seal glowed with a sunburst and whispered my name when I touched it.

That was the day I left behind what I knew, and I stepped into a world that was bigger, harder, and full of magic I didn't yet understand.

Guild Assignments

On my first day at Ninth Realm, they gathered us into a big hall with floating banners. There were five of them, swirling high above, changing shape and color with every moment.

I waited in a long line as students were sorted. Some cheered. Others groaned.

Then Headmistress Avalora floated into the room, eyes sharp as a sword tip. She unrolled her scroll, which rolled far beyond anybody's sight.

"Danrik Middle…Middle…Middlemere, you're in… Emberfang Guild."

Whispers followed. I knew Emberfang was the toughest guild, the one that always had the most challenges and the least mercy.

Still, as the banner flared red and gold above me, I stood tall. I was ready. At least I thought I was.

Homework in the Flame Tower

The Flame Tower was Emberfang's home quarters. Its walls were made of enchanted brick that shimmered when you were nervous (which I often was).

Mistress Avalora wasted no time. "Three scrolls," she said, "on ancient wand theory, one incantation translation, two potion reactions."

I barely finished reading the assignment when she added, "Due at moonrise."

My desk was covered in scrolls with notes. My parchment was worn and wrinkled. My head felt foggy, and my brain felt like it had been hit by a sleep spell.

But when I turned in my scroll, I saw a flicker of approval in her eyes.

It was small. But it meant everything.

The Concert of Echoes

I thought music class would be relaxing.

Then I met Mistress Doyliana. Her classroom floated.
Instruments hovered mid-air. Notes danced like fireflies.

"Your spell-song must not only be sung, it must be felt," she told
us.

I struggled. When nervous, my voice cracked and my wand
sparked.

For the Concert of Echoes, we had to perform in front of the
entire school, the harmonies had to be woven with magic.

I was terrified. But I practiced under the moonlight, humming
the tune again and again.

On concert night, my voice trembled, but the spell took shape.

 And the room filled with light.

The Broom Test

Flying sounded fun until I tried it.
Sir Illkar was a former sky-knight. His armor still clicked when
he walked. He stood next to our rows of brooms with a scowl.

 "Mount, Lift, Hover." Easier said than done.

I fell. A lot. Once, my broom spun me upside down until I landed
in the bushes that were filled with Cindernits, they are the little
pesky bugs that, when they get on your clothes light up.

After extinguishing my robe and laughing with my classmates, I tried again and again.

I practiced late into the dusk. I whispered encouragement to my broom. I learned its rhythm.

On test day, I soared.

Not high. Not fast. But steady.

And that was enough to earn my wings and fly towards enlightenment with one less goal on my list.

Acting with Master Croalus

Master Croalus never walked he glided. His cape followed like a shadow. The Theater of Illusion, we didn't just act, we conjured the stories with magic.

"Your illusion must breathe with the emotion of the scene," he said.

I was cast as the lost prince. I had to cry on cue, cast a mirror-spell, and speak in old rune language.

I tripped over the words at first. My mirror cracked.

But I stayed in character.

By the final line, the illusion held.

And the best and warmest moment was when the rising hall started filling with applause.

Potions Challenge in the Cauldron Wing

Professor Liggenmoor taught potions in the deepest part of the school, where the ceilings dripped and the air smelled like mandragora roots. He was tall, thin, and had a beard that looked like it had once been on fire.

"Your task," he said, tapping a bubbling cauldron with his wand, "is to brew Flamevine Elixir. One mistake, and your robe may never recover." as soon as he finished his sentence, his eyes fell on me, and in his glare it was readable that he was talking about me.

I followed the instructions carefully until a bug landed on my sleeve. It was a Cindernit.

I panicked, and petrified it before my sleeve could turned into ash, fortunately Cindernit fell right into my position, and seeing my potion turnning green was the number 1999 reason why I could have ended up in the school's hospital for several weeks.

Liggenmoor didn't blink, and with a small smile, whispered to me, "Better than most," handing me a patch for my robe.

 Somehow, I passed.

Magical Away Games

The first away match was terrifying.

We rode sky-carriages to Frostspire Academy—known for its icy magic and colder attitudes.

I was our shield caster. My job? Protect the team from curses and spell-bolts.

Their team was brutal. The sky howled. My wand burned in my hand.

We lost that match barely, and it stung. The team had their heads down, including me, but our captain, Zanther, stepped up and gave a speech that everybody on the team needed. At that moment, our magical bus exploded with cheers and motivational spirits.

We trained hard. We fixed our formations and strengthened our spells. In our second match against Emberwell Spire, we fought like one.

I blocked three attacks. My shield shimmered like dragon glass. The attacks from Ericson were piercing the opponent's defense.

We won, we did it, the happiness we all felt was greater than anything I ever witnessed before.

I earned my Emberfang badge that day not for perfection, but for standing alongside my team.

Making Friends & More

I didn't know anyone when I arrived.

Everyone seemed to have their own circle, their own magic language. I sat alone at meals.

Studied in silence. Then I met Kaelin—a bower from Starleaf

Guild. She trained in nature magic and archery, often alone.

She let me join. We practiced. Shared stories. Failed and laughed.

She wasn't flashy, but she was kind.

And suddenly, the Ninth Realm felt less like a dungeon.

More like... home.

The Tests That Broke Me

Lady Kaurana had sharp eyes, the longest and the hardest tests.

She gave us mind-riddles, logic spells, and math that moved across the page. I failed my first test. Completely.

But she didn't scold me. She just said, "Return stronger." So I did. I studied under starlight, asked for help, and rewrote my notes three times. And on the next test, my quill glowed gold when I finished.

I passed, not with ease, but with effort.

And that meant more.

Who I Am Now Now

I walk the Emberfang halls with steady steps.

I remember Middlemere. I miss Lady Phamira's warm cloak and Sir Randor's booming tales.

But I've grown.

I've faced windstorms, wandfailures, loneliness, and pressure.

I've soared, stumbled, sung, and stood tall.

I am Danrik. Of Emberfang.

And this is just the beginning.

Qi'yanna Lemon

Qi'yanna Lemon is a student at WISH Academy High School who enjoys writing encouraging and uplifting poems that help people feel seen. She began writing when she got a writing assignment in the third grade to create a narrative. When not writing, Qi'yanna likes to play soccer, volleyball, watch movies/shows, and play with animals. This is her first published story.

In his Image
by Qi'yanna Lemon

I'm that girl with the brown skin,
The girl who has hair as big as the motherland.
Whispers all around me, it's happening again,
I can't understand.

I'm either too dark or too light,
either way I'm in your sight
I see you peeking, I hear you speaking
Yet I still keep my chin held high.

My skin glistens like gold,
yet you still whisper,
Tell me why?
Why does my skin and hair attract?
As if it is an artifact.
Why does my mane bring a frown,
When it's only my crown?

My beautiful brown skin and my thick hair,
Stands firm against all whispers!

I AM that girl!

That girl with the beautiful brown skin.
That girl with the big black hair.
That girl who never stands down because I am aware!
Aware that I am made perfectly.
Perfectly in his image.

I AM that girl!

Jessica Malayil

Jessica Malayil is a student at WISH Academy High School who enjoys writing (and reading) fiction, fantasy and adventure stories. She began writing stories back in 7th grade when she was required to write a fiction story for an anthology in 7th grade. She soon realized how fun writing could be. She likes her writing to perfect, and will keep rewriting, and changing the story until it is. Unfortunately, this time she changed the story too many times and had no time to fix her final story to her liking. When not writing, Jessica Malayil likes to read. This is her 3rd and most disliked published story.

The End of the World ????
by Jessica Malayil

God, I hate running, but boy was it helpful now. Never in my life have I been so thankful for track. When I first found out my parents signed me up for the "sport," I flipped. Now, I wish I had just thanked them for it, but they're gone. Missing, to be more exact. I mean, everyone is. You see, a couple of weeks ago a journalist found out about the U.S. military's attempts to genetically modify a Deinocheirus in order to create an urban siege beast. And you imagine it went well—HORRIBLY WRONG! I mean, have you seen Jurassic Park? Hold on, let me start from the beginning.

You see, a couple of weeks ago, I was sitting on my bed, shrouded in blankets and comforters, trying to keep warm in the winter cold when I got a strange notification on my phone. I picked it up and took a quick look. It was the small influencer named Tune In that I follow on YouTube. She was some anonymous journalist of sorts. She would never show her face or her body, just talked through a strange voice modulator. I liked her content though. I mean, a lot of it was conspiracy theories, but who are you to say those aren't a valid source of information?

 Anyways, she had just uploaded a new video called The End of the World????. It seemed interesting enough, so I clicked on it. It started off like this:

"Listen, I don't know how many of you are tuning in right now, and I don't know how many of you will tune in before it's too late. But if you're here, then listen up. I know it sounds crazy, but the U.S. military is hiding a lot more than you think they are. We all know of the genetic modification of fruits and animals. But what about modification on EXTINCT animals? We all know that scientists have been trying to bring back extinct animals for a long while now, but the reason for doing such a thing can't just be because of pity on the poor animals we massacred. It has to have more to it. So I did some digging around at the PENTAGON, and you won't believe what I found. Plans. Project Thanatostris. Project Thanatostris is a plan to genetically modify an extinct animal, the Deinocheirus. Except this isn't just normal genetic modification. No, they planned on turning it into a whole different breed, Deinocheirus Mortifex. Its modifications would include increased speed to a whopping 20 miles per hour, enlarged claws created to be even more durable than titanium, armored skin, Hive uplink compatibility, hemotoxic blood, regenerative, increased intelligence... the list goes on. If I were to read you the full lab report, we would be here all day. What's worse about this situation is that they have already created IT. Well, attempts have at least been made. The reports keep saying that they need to tone down its aggression and increase loyalty. I doubt we have much time before sci-fi becomes reality. Well, my audience—"

And that's all that I remember from the video. Don't judge me for forgetting—how would I know that information from a dumb vlog would be helpful now! Moving on, somehow that ended up being her least viewed video. It actually got reported four days after it was posted for "false news" and got taken down.

Exactly two weeks from when that was posted, news articles

began reporting an unidentified animal breaking down protected forest land in the area. The footprints found were about 3 feet, much larger than any normal animal could make.

Now I'm not a conspiracy theory believer, but even I was starting to question it. The issue soon cleared up after two guys admitted to creating the footprints as a small prank.

But only 24 hours after that statement, my grandad calls. And he NEVER calls. Not unless something is wrong.

My mom picks up the phone and puts it on speaker (I was told no phones at the dinner table, but I guess the "rules" are different for her). He begins to anxiously ramble over the line. He kept saying:

"The monster, the monster, it's here."

Now, my mom kinda, might've thought my grandad had lost it. I mean, he's been living alone out in the country for quite some time now. A look of concern washed over her. She quickly flipped on the mute button and turned to start talking to my dad. Something about how they need to start taking care of him. I blocked them out and decided to zone into my grandad's rambles.

"I saw it! It was so tall and large, it had armored skin, large claws, it made a large booming sound! So loud, it was so loud!" he screamed.

I'd hate to agree with my mom, but it does kinda sound like he lost it.

"My crops, it destroyed my crops! My livestock! They're gone! It disappeared into the woods!" he cried.

My mom quickly picked up the phone, telling him everything would be ok and that we would be there by tomorrow morning.

Wait, WHAT!

I quickly interject, saying, "Excuse me! Why the heck are we heading toward the danger?! Did you not just hear him say that there was a giant beast out there?!"

My mom quickly signals me to shush before getting back on the line with my grandad. My dad gets out of his worn-out wooden chair to come squat down next to me. The chair squeaks… along with his knees.

"Hey," he says softly, "I know it seems silly to head towards the place where there's 'danger,' but your grandad isn't the most reliable source of information. He's getting old, Kasey. His brain isn't really all that there anymore." I deadpan.

"You speak to me as if I'm 10. I'm 15! Yes, I know that grandad isn't all that there anymore, but why risk it! This is too elaborate for him to just be lying about it!" I exclaim, desperately trying to convince him of how bad of an idea this is. It's too eerily similar to Tune In's video.

"Well, is it really lying if he thinks it's the truth? Whatever. We have to go tomorrow. Grandad needs us. So pack whatever you'll need for a couple of days and we'll head out in an hour," he says firmly, leaving no room for further comments.

I turn around, ready to trek to my room.

"Oh," my dad starts again, "and please stop listening to sci-fi. I think it's all getting into your head," my dad joked.

I groaned and then angrily walked off to my room, purposefully stomping loudly (well, as loud as I could) on each carpeted step, making sure they knew how I felt about their decision. I finally reach the door of my room. Forgetting how light it is, I swing it open a bit too hard and it slams against the wall. I ignore it and just head inside and start to pack.

An hour later, Mom calls me out of my room, telling me that it's time to go, and I quickly grab my backpack, turn off the light, and make my way downstairs into the living room, where my Mom and Dad were already ready to go.

We swiftly file out the front door before locking it and getting into our car. My Dad gets into the driver's seat, and my mom in the passenger's seat. I get into the back seat of the car and begin to strap myself in.

"It's gonna be a long 3-hour ride to Grandad's farm. Just be prepared," my dad chuckles.

He starts to pull out of the driveway. We launch into our long journey to Grandad's. I put on my headphones and begin to listen to soft music. I stare out the window at the passing trees and houses, praying that my suspicions are wrong. I begin to fall asleep to the soft music and rocking of the car.

Our car began to approach Grandad's property when a sudden

thud jolted me awake. Suddenly Tune In's video comes to mind. A thousand different thoughts race through.

"Mom, did you feel that?" I jump forward in my seat, desperately trying to find out if I'm crazy. "Feel what? I didn't feel anything," my mom replies, clearly confused.

"Dad, what about you? Did you feel that thud?" I ask once more. "I—I… think you're reading too many stories," he chortles at his own joke.

I roll my eyes at his antics. I go back to looking at my phone, trying to forget what I "thought" I heard earlier. Though I still take off my headphones just in case I need to be alert.

About 30 seconds later, I hear a large rustling sound from the forest behind Grandad's property. I turn to look and I see—

To be continued...

Kai McGregor

Kai McGregor is a student at WISH Academy High School who enjoys marine biology, musicals, the horror genre, psychology, and the craft of writing. She began writing when she was in the first grade, scribbling pictures and words down into composition books to form creative and elaborate stories. When not writing, Kai likes to analyze her favorite characters, ones from favorite games and also her own. This is her first published story.

Little Flower
by Kai McGregor

"...There you are." Saffron's mother carefully tied the two ends of her son's sizable neck kerchief together, forming a secure and brilliant bow that erupted vivaciously to the side. She latched onto the outsides of his arms, swiftly wheeling him around to begin properly studying her handiwork. A large, proud, and beaming grin spread like fire across her face while a rough and weathered hand found its place on his magnificently fluffy head. "You look wonderful, anak ko."

Saffron, standing up straight, now fully suited with his usual patterned scarf, held ample affection for his mother. Though he was not good at it–and arguably terrible–he curved the edges of his lips upward into a poor attempt at imitating the show of immense joy and pride being displayed to him. He spent hours at a time in the mirror on some days attempting to craft the perfect smile, hoping and praying to eliminate at least one of several reasons he was tyrannized by his peers. But most of all, even above his need to escape the constant harassment at school, he wanted a smile truly befitting of the only one who took the time to take care of him all his life: floral virtuoso, Cecilia Croce.
The mother and son tightly held a session of prolonged eye contact, almost as if they were communicating inside their heads. Nothing breathing or inanimate dared to make even a whisper in their quiet home. There were no ticking clocks, primarily due to an incident where Saffron would not stop screaming and crying because of the awful and painfully unchanging noise knocking on his fragile ears, no dreadful whirring of fluorescent light bulbs,

and not a single droplet of rebellious water making its escape from any faucet. They continued to stare, submerging themselves deeper into the other's mind. There was no way to describe the unimaginably strong bond between Ms. Croce and her son. They were somehow connected by the soul.

The teenager blinked twice and received a combination of three blinks, a warm closed-mouth smile, and a nod in response. What he wordlessly informed her was that he was ready to head out, and she had sweetly replied to him: "Be safe." Hesitantly, he walked backwards, still looking directly at her face. It was naturally painted with differently sized dark splotches. Often it was that he thought of his mother as nature's canvas. Saffron waved goodbye to her one last time and quickened his pace, walking with not the slightest bit of urgency through the vibrant and flashy colors of the garden that he raised mostly alone since he was ten or eleven. Gardening was his passion, likely because of his mom and her expertise in floral arrangements.

One reason that Saffron was harassed so much and so relentlessly in school would be his extreme closeness with his parent–and having just one parent at all–as an almost sixteen-year-old sophomore in high school. Most kids in his grade laughed about easily exploiting and mistreating their own, and every time he overheard them, it annoyed him nearly enough to make him–a remarkably social skill deficient individual–raise his voice. He was extremely thankful that it hadn't happened, painfully aware that they would only laugh their lives away at him. All he could do was silently pray and beg to never grow into something like that; a monster towards his Ina.

Going to school was painful having lost Atlantis two years ago and Poppy two years before that. He was now utterly devoid of security, and his classmates had somehow even less desire to

acquaint themselves with him. He was to them–and he slowly
began to believe it himself–a sort of evil eye; a curse. Saffron's
classmates referred to him with many cruel names, but none of
them ever got to him more than "sow and reaper." He would
happily accept the title with its connection to his passions if it
was for anything but the double meaning they intended.

So lost in thought, Saffron had not realized–until shoved by
eagerly speeding children spilling out of the bus–that he was in
front of his towering school building. Oh, how he really dreaded
this place. As he carefully toed towards the large doors, he
couldn't help but compare himself to a head of cattle voluntarily
waltzing into the slaughterhouse.
The situations were not so different.

Saffron walked heavily through his school's congested hallway,
his shoulders nudging those of people he could not even see. He
despised attending a large school more than anything.
Regardless, he vowed to make sure his caregiver would never
hear that from him. His senescent mother worked extremely
hard at her several and unpredictable jobs, arriving back late at
night completely spent. On occasion, she did not arrive home
that same day at all. He could not even imagine what sorts of
jobs she worked, but clearly, they were difficult. Saffron
remembered all too well one night pleading with his mother–
bedded with scars on her face and hands–to let him go to work in
place of her and even worse, the unforgettable angry tears she
cried as she forbade him. He was thankful for her early off days
and the ones she had free for him, such as today. It saved him the
worry, but it did not lift his spirits by much. She was home for
the entire day today while he was stuck at this awful, hellish,

misery-inducing place. Though impossible, he wished he had savored the weekend somehow more than usual.

The fifteen-year-old was not paying attention at all to where he was going, all too familiar with the path to his destination that he'd taken for years. His legs grudgingly carried him to the front of his first class' hollow metal door, mercilessly coated with countless and multicolored indecent scribbles.

Saffron yelped as he swiftly dodged the harshly swinging open door. The culprit quickly revealed herself, a girl of average height who looked about his age. She was furious and made that fact crystal clear by loudly groaning and stomping even louder down the hall to hopefully her own locker—as she kicked it almost hard enough to make a dent. Saffron recognized her as Giselle Fox from his now deceased close friend's old rival soccer team. The reason for her anger became evident shortly enough after as she whipped out her violently buzzing phone. Accepting the call, she screamed into the speaker. "What the hell do you want now?!" Saffron slipped stealthily into the classroom and raced to his assigned seat. That particular chair and its placement were high on his list of things he hated most, but he was willing to kiss the permanently cold and graffiti-stained seat of it to avoid being used as a punching bag to vent out his classmate's patent and potent rage.

"For you to get back in this classroom so I can beat your—!" The person on the other line—a man famously denied graduation—who, as Saffron noted, appeared to be her new boyfriend for the week—shouted unnecessarily into the phone.

"Oh, I wish you would, Tristan." Giselle ignored the long string of foul words alongside her name from her boyfriend and scoffed. A few scattered gasps sounded throughout the room. Anyone who had a will to live called him 'T', even in thinking so as to never make the mistake that she just did. The T in question stood up in such a way that one could swear he'd set off an earthquake if his moves were just slightly more aggressive. He slammed his balled-up hands on the table, sending his expensive phone to the ground with a thud.

"That's enough!" Ms. Clark finally yelled, as if she couldn't take any action several minutes before. Though Saffron held much hatred for her, he understood her position. Even if she did try to stop them before, no one respected her quite enough to care. However, in her case, it was almost completely her fault. "Everyone sit down!" Her hoarse voice with a slight audible tremor fell on a crowd of deaf ears.

T bolted through the classroom door, fixated on catching Giselle and inferably pummeling her into the hard tile floor. Saffron recalled T doing that very thing to him the week prior after he refused to give him something of his to impress that same girl. He was terribly injured and entirely alone that night, besides his cat who curled up beside him until he fell asleep. Remembering that dreadful day made him shudder and subconsciously begin rubbing the bony area above his cheek where he landed smack on. The combination of screaming and clanging of lockers as they were hit against was impressively louder than the roaring chaos Ms. Clark's room had been sent into. The phone was still on speaker lying on the floor, providing anyone with ears a loud and clear medium for listening in–for better or worse.

"God, he's gonna kill her." One of the students spoke quietly to another, laughing despite the perceptible horror in his voice.

"Yeah. Her fault, though." They both shrugged. What could they possibly do? Despite the obvious fact that no one was listening, Ms. Clark explained the math formulas that she prepared on the board before class in her foul, sour voice. Her lanky fingers wrapped firmly around her twig-like rod, directing not a soul's attention to the sections she was discussing. With one final piercing and obscenity-loaded screech, the banging abruptly stopped. T returned with a smug look on his face.

"Well?" He spat on the floor, making condescending eye contact with several other kids, melting them into terrified puddles in their seats. "Still believe that snake kid's your king?" Ms. Clark groaned, physically repulsed by the disgusting glob on her room's floor as if that was the worst of things down there.

Every person in the room looked around at one another and whispered. When discussing the title of "king" of the school and who it could be attributed to, two people came to mind immediately: Nyoka and T. One was a Machiavellian charmer, and the other a shameless tyrant. Both indefinitely cruel. Saffron, or the "cursed boy" as they called him, was plagued by their friends–though "disciples" was a more accurate word–in some way every day he showed his face on campus.

The teacher gave up, sitting herself down and immediately sinking into her rolling chair. Her life was nothing to be envied. After the recent divorce that ripped everything she loved violently away from her, even her old-aged children hadn't spoken to her in months. The kids she taught despised and disrespected her, she wasn't paid well enough to live a full life at her ripe old age of sixty-four… It would only be a matter of time, she thought, though she couldn't put in words exactly what it was.

The bell signaling the end of the school day rang, finally, and the students began flooding the halls, racing through them like a crazed stampede of bulls. Saffron stayed back in the classroom, waiting behind to discuss his grades with Ms. Clark. He advanced prudently towards her desk, shoving his anxiety behind him before speaking. "Hello."

She was lost in her own thoughts and did not realize he was even there. Saffron cleared his throat and spoke once more. "...Hello?"

The instructor flinched. "Hello?" Realizing who it was, her muscles relaxed and she immediately became irritated. "What?"

Saffron sighed. There was no reason for her to be so forward about how much she couldn't stand him. It was much too clear that she saw him exclusively as an idiot, thanks to his accommodation plan that she so skillfully turned a blind eye to. Needing it at all took a toll on him on its own. "...I need you to explain a lesson to me..." He coughed, "...so I can retake a test." Ms. Clark took in a sharp breath. She wanted so badly to refuse him, but perhaps it would feel good to have someone pay attention to her for once.

"Alright."

The fifteen-year-old boy spent about half an hour more than necessary time in his teacher's classroom. Swallowing every single word she said, he forced himself to retain every piece of information before being handed the familiar sheet of paper.

Ms. Clark was amazed when the page was returned to her in ten minutes with much nicer results than when it was assigned a week ago.

"...Great work."

As Saffron left the room, she could not help but grin, really feeling the pulses of pride and success that coursed throughout her entire body. At the same time, her eyes were watering as she was too aware that this feeling was temporary, like a drug. It was gone by the time she sat in her old rusty car that refused to start for seven whole minutes before she could begin driving the long and contemplation-filled road home. However, she was smiling the entire time. She finally knew what it was. She finally understood. It was finally time.

Ms. Clark arrived in her parking lot, bubbling out of the car, and flinging open the door to her cold, dark, and desolate home with no regard for closing it behind her. It was a sizable house, but what was the use if there was no longer anyone to share it with? She practically flew towards her computer, the dim brightness from the monitor lighting up the room. It was open to one very specific email. She never had the courage to send it as she never dared to do what she implied. However, today was a special day. She happily hit the 'send' key, mass forwarding the long message she had been saving for months, with only one revision: her sign-off. Her own and last little act of rebellion.

Beaming, she abandoned her device and headed for the bedroom. On a typical day, she carefully picked out each pill from their respective cavity and placed them into her hand to be sure she was taking her proper dosages. Again, today was different. She scanned the labels on the circular container until she found the one she was looking for. "Five hundred milligrams, pain medication, extra strength. Take no more than three as needed." She processed the words her primary care provider nailed into her brain often shortly after he became in contact with her therapist.

In spite, she hastily shook the entirety of the nearly overflowing compartment into her palm and clasped the same hand over her open mouth, downing the contents all at the same time. That day, she learned the pills she was prescribed for her aching body were perfect for the ache of existing as well. Her mouth, chin, and neck were quickly bathing in a deadly effervescence.

The following day at school–and only for that day–Saffron was lauded and praised. His peers treated him almost kindly and not all of them were being mocking. He didn't understand at all, incredibly alarmed and confused until he checked his phone. His eyes widened. Apparently, his curse struck the right person this time.

Thanks for nothing, and goodbye.
– Amelia Clark.

Mariah Morales

Mariah Morales is a student at WISH Academy High School who enjoys reading novels and writing about things others may connect with. She began writing as a coping skill when she was at the age of 9. She began writing as her way of expressing her emotions and now hopes to provide a feeling of comfort for others through her writing. When not writing, Mariah likes to train and play soccer, read, and go out with friends. This is her first published story however, she plans on publishing more of her own work in the future.

Thoughts
by Mariah Morales

Alone

being alone
the peace that comes with it
being able to be on ur own
feeling at ease with yourself
being able to recharge your
mind feeling alone
whats the difference?
feeling alone
the feeling of no one
the loneliness of urself
the thoughts overwhelming your mind
the presence of others but not the
comfort the difference between the
two
being alone is peace
being alone is comfort
being alone is care
feeling alone is torture
feeling alone is no one
feeling alone is no support
alone is both a light and a dark
Alone.

the Spark

i was sparkless
unheard and unseen
i was a complete mess
there was no spark
i was completely in the dark
a flame approaches me
the flame that happened to be you the
flame that sparked back my eyes the
eyes that once cried
i was heard
i was seen
the spark returned and flew high like a
bird your presence started the spark
now i can grow to be my own
herd the herd in my own heart
you empower it and make it
grow just as u did with my s
park.

See Through

Time passed and people knew
They saw but did they see
through The mask and act that
was used
When really I was internally
bruised Months and months of therapy
to heal really healing for
me feels unreal
People see me but do they see through
I'm tired and want to feel something
new Do I even feel anything anymore
Sitting on the bathroom floor
the thoughts that come to mind
the actions that are unkind
not to others but to myself
Maybe I'll learn to forget
For the time being I'll keep the mask
& act So people see me
They see what's visible
They don't see what isn't
They see me but don't see through me.

Change

you left that day with satisfaction
i left with a heavy heart
the hands that brought me safety
became the ones i hid from
you said it was love
when really u were full of
cravings cravings i wish i
never met
the eyes that i was lost in
became the ones i never want to meet a
gain the words that once brought me
comfort became the words that guilted
me guilted me for satisfaction
not of my own but satisfaction i never
wanted what was your pleasure
became my biggest fear

dear lover

In the time we had I saw
dear lover
in another lifetime i will find you
i will find you and heal you
the way i should have in this lifetime
dear lover
ill commit and promise to you
promise to love and care for you
dear lover
in another lifetime i'll do what i should've now
i'll love you the way I should've known how.

A Page of Grief

I was once told, "to love and to be loved is to feel the sun from both sides". i however was the moon during an eclipse blocking u from feeling one side of the sun. my side of the sun was blocked out by the moon. the moon full of things that didn't allow myself to be loved the way u loved me. The sun was almost completely covered by the eclipse when I was ready to be a part of the sun again.

the morning After

the morning after,
the birds chirp the same and the sun rises
my bed left undone and my room left uncleaned
everything seems the same but nothing feels the same
My mom is laying on her bed wondering how she didn't notice
her daughter was dying from depression. my aunts wondering
how they never saw any signs
my aunt thinking maybe if she helped more i would have been
here
my cat waiting for me to come out the bathroom meowing like
she always does
my grandparents unable to get up from their bed in pain and
agony
my friends wondering how they could have stopped me
my little cousin crying out of confusion and denial.
I left everything the way it was before.
nor did i give my stuff away
subtle but obvious sign that tonight was it
i didn't speak to anyone that day
maybe it would've helped them i thought
My voice gone one day
The next, my soul too
the morning after,
Silence

Unheard

The words i never spoke
Unspoken like a secret left untold
The heart wrenching feeling
Words that filled my heart with
mold But oh how a word could
change it all The silence that i
never broke
Maybe they would make me fall
The thoughts and words left untold
The feeling of what could be
difference Maybe if i spoke out
more
The wrenched feeling gone
For now i remain unheard
Maybe in the future i could be
louder Louder like a bird
Unheard.

the color white in a box of colors.

The crayon that goes unnoticed and
unused. The color that seems to have no
purpose The silenced and unseen
 Unseen like an ant on the floor.
The color of nothing
The color white
The color that brings light to
others. It allows others to shine
Shine like the moon on the dark blue
night The purpose of the color white
The change of tone and vibrance
The way the color enhances
The purposeful color of white.
I learned that I am the color
white. At first I was unseen and
unnoticed. The color that was
shut out
Later i learned i was a spark
A spark in others
A spark that helped others grow
I was the color white in a box of colors
The color white.

Treyce Turner

Treyce Turner is a student at WISH Academy High School who enjoys writing fiction stories and poems. He began writing after taking Ms. Avalos' English class, where she inspired me to tell my own stories. When not writing, Treyce Turner likes to hang out with friends. This is his first published story.

im scared.

by Treyce Turner

i'm scared,
I drown in the thought of the future,
fearful of growing up.
The weight of tomorrow feels
too heavy on my mind,
like a headache I can't seem to get rid
of, Pulsing at the rhythm of a drum.
I'm afraid,
horrified by the silence
that chases the blank noise,
of the choices I have made
and decisions I can't undo.
The world is constantly spinning
As I sit still,
questioning if I'll ever
have the ability to move.
Time whirrs in my ear and distorts in my eyes
As if it knows and sees something I don't A
 vision I'm too blind to see,
A vision I'm too observant to ignore.
A secret I'm too young to hear,
A secret I'm too old to brush off.
I try to breathe in,
But suddenly the air feels different,
thicker with questions
No on can ever seem to answer.

Grace Velasco

Grace Velasco is a student at WISH Academy High School who enjoys "exploring human emotions through fiction,". She began writing during the COVID years. When not writing, Grace likes to read and watch shows.
This is her first published story.

Verses From My Veins
by Grace Velasco

The story of coming into this world is that you find out the struggles later.
You're going to become a daughter and grow into a woman.
But you don't know that.
You're crying because opening your eyes is all a new thing.
Seeing your mom smile at you and tell you your name.
It's new.
You were so used to the comfort of the womb.
The comfort of the blurred-out noise, constant meals, and the comfort of your mother's voice.
But now, change has to happen.
You need to step into the next level of your future.
Take it in.
Don't take it for granted.
Soothe yourself in the comfort of your mother's arms.
Listen to the beat of her heart.
Live in the moment.

In your years of adolescence, you have fun.
You live and cry like there is no tomorrow.
You're in love with your mother.
See her as a superhero on TV.
You get older and find out she was in deep pain.
But no need to learn that yet.
Your parents are separated.
You see your dad every weekend.

Get traumatized from some of the moments with him.
Not because of him.
No.
Because of that woman.
Wait, I've spilled too much.
Hold back your tongue.
Keep your mouth closed.
And smile.
You carry on with your days and moments of happiness.
You see the cracks of your mother crying.
Keeping to herself.
No, let's close that crack up.
Let us not see it.
Keep it together as long as possible.
Your sister was your anchor at the time.
She took care of you while maintaining her problems.
Later, you'll find out she was also in deep pain in her teenage years.
But no need to learn that yet.
Too young.
Carry on with those glimpses of happiness you remember.
Don't look at what you aren't meant to see.

In a few more years, you're in deep pain.
Well, you don't know that yet.
You think it's part of growing up.
And it is, but your experience was worse.
COVID hit you like a brick in the head.
You were always so cheery and happy as a kid.
But once it hit you, it hit you hard.

The shadows in your head are telling you how to feel.
The darkness in your room and mind covered up all the light.
The blood spilling out of your head when alone.
The blood spilling from your thighs down.
The itch to see light.
The itch to want to sleep forever.
At 9.
At 9, my life turned upside down.
It had been tilting, but it was never down.
Now, in these years, it had finally turned upside down.
It was a time of growing fast.
Growing when I should've been playing with dolls.
Shouldn't have been thinking of the darkness.
Nor should she have been thinking what it would be like not to
live.
Devastating.
To think she was so gone.
 Not her.
Not the girl she used to be.
She grew so fast.
Left her childhood in a matter of years.
Yet she never questioned it, even when she should have.
She didn't know any better.
She was slightly broken.
Slightly cracked.
She knew something was wrong with herself.
But didn't know what.
She was getting into trouble year by year.
Till the age of 12.
Wait, I've gone too far.
Grace, stay in the present.

Please don't drift too far.
You'll only hurt yourself more.
Sorry. Back to where I was. My ninth year of age was tragic.
Everything changed.

After her 4 years of dread came to a stop, her life saw hope.
She saw her dreams on a silver platter.
But it wasn't in arm's reach.
No, it was way up high in a cloud.
She knew she had to climb and climb and climb.
She knew she wouldn't make it.
Well, at least not yet.
She built her life step by step.
Helped herself feel better.
Her mother was there for her in ways her father wasn't.
She couldn't see him for 4 years.
She always wanted communication with him, yet didn't know
how to ask for it.
Of course, it hits her now and in the future.
Doesn't know how to communicate.
Doesn't know how to express her opinion.
Say how she feels.
She can't open her mouth and say,
I'm not ok.
She can't admit that she wishes her life were different at times.
She wishes that life were easier.
That maybe, she won't have to suffer for anyone but herself.
But she's a people pleaser after all.
She doesn't know how to care for herself at a time when she
should.

Oh, sorry, I'm losing track again.
Back to the story.
She had a best friend who dragged her to the ground.
But of course, her eyes were too blind to see that it was toxic.
Her mother got her out of the situation.
Encouraged every bit of her to stand up for herself.
It hurt her mother to see her daughter get mistreated by
someone who didn't treat her well.
Someone who made her feel awful for who she was.
It took time for her daughter to see.
To see that it was not ok.
To see that she was being mistreated.
It hurt her to see that her best friend was not the girl she once
loved with all her heart.
That it was no longer us.
But you.
And me.
Separate people.
No longer connected by the memories of the past.

So she lost her.
She finally chose for herself.
She finally saw through new eyes.
And finally, she wanted to see herself bloom.

A year ago from today, she can admit.
She was in a bad place.
She got into trouble again.
Felt awful.
Felt lost.

She had achieved one of her goals.
She was so proud.
But of course, she messed it up.
She lost herself once again.
But this time she's not going to sit in a puddle of tears.
No, she's going to make it up to herself. She's going to achieve
her goals with as much passion as she can.
Even if it breaks her in the process.
She will come out even stronger. And be the girl she hoped her
younger self could see.

She dreams of love in her sleep.
Dreams of what it's like to be held in the arms of someone she
loves.
Hopes that one day she'll find it.
Find her forever.
Maybe now, maybe later.

But on day.
And when se does, hopefully, he doesn't become her darkness,
too.
She has too many.
She doesn't want him to be one, too.
She hopes her love looks at her like this time, she is the light.
Too much to ask for?
Maybe.
But wished and dreams come true.

Grace, your doing good.
Don't put pressure on yourself to be perfect.

No such thing as perfect.
Don't stress.
Oh, my darling, don't cry.
Don't shed unnecessary tears.
You're trying your hardest.
And you're doing way more than what you planned.
Give yourself credit.
Oh, I'm sorry!
I'm not supposed to speak.
I'll plaster my smile back on.
That's what you're meant to see.
Back to the story of the present.
She's stressed.
Crying.
Day by Day.
But this time, she sees through the tears.
She's not going to stay in her head and rethink every single
little detail.
She's going to try till she can't.
She's going to reach her dreams.
She's going to do what her mother knew she could.
But this time for herself.
She's finally going to please herself.
See what her younger self couldn't see.
Hopefully, she doesn't break again.
But she is more likely will.
And that's ok.

She's human after all.
And no one is perfect.

Theori Vickers

Theori Vickers is a student at WISH Academy High School, 24-25, who enjoys Dystopian literary works such as The Electric State, the book's inspiration. This dude began writing at age 10 when he was asked to write a short story about one of the books he read in class. He turned in feeling proud of the work that took only a few hours, kick-starting a journey to publish books. After a few years of writing multiple concept stories, he finally published a short story based on the disappearance of the SS Pacific, which he mistook for the Atlantic in a school anthology. The next year, he began work on a yet-to-be-finished book coming out in who knows when. Now he is the proud story writer of the hit book Static Shock. When not writing, Theori Vickers likes to play Rocket League, TF2, Dragon Ball R, Brawlhalla, HOI4, brick rigs, drift paradise, BMG, soccer (football), and go-kart racing. This is Theori Vickers' second "finished" published story.

Static Shocked

by Theori Vickers

(Inspired by The Electric State by Simon Stalenhag)

Section 1 (Who do you think?)

Recent message:
"Hey Tom, it's me, Jennifer—just calling to ask if you're feeling any better. I know the flu has been flying around lately and everyone at school is getting really sick. Yeah, we may not know each other well, but as the head of student council, it is my job to check on everyone—and I mean everyone—in school. So, best of wishes from your number one Ms. Council Superstar."
—Jennifer Hocking

You know what it feels like to wake up in a bed that isn't your own, yet still feels so familiar? Well, never could I have guessed this strange question would be my life for what feels like eternity. Waking up for the first time was a bit of a pain. Having no memory of why I was randomly in a bed with grey-covered sheets and with distinct smell of expired milk freaked me out so much I ran screaming for fifty whole minutes before finally calming down cause who wouldn't when in a room that wasn't yours.

You'd think the first thoughts of someone in a position similar to mine would be "What? Where? How?" or some other arbitrary thoughts racing through the mind. However, being a nothing-burger with barely above-average grades—a teenager who felt like they were dying for the last two weeks—I smirked and looted the clearly abandoned house for whatever it had.

Funnily enough, I managed to find a backpack with food, some baggy and "standard"-looking clothes, a pistol-looking weapon that doesn't have a mag (nor a place to put one), a few notebooks, and a phone that looked quite similar to mine—though it doesn't seem to have any signal, so it's useless. Besides a bullet vest and a hat, there wasn't much else. After putting on the vest, hat, and jacket, I left the house in search of a signal so I could call someone to get me out of wherever I happened to be.

My eyes were met with a gloomy sky as I stepped onto yellow, wheat-colored grass—foreign to Phoenix. Felt like I was in another state—maybe northern Texas, I thought to myself, continuing down into the grassy area. The only things in what was probably a local town were boxy, greyish houses that got lighter the from down the house, with single-paned windows that still had lights on. Yet no one seemed to be in any of them.

A.k.a., either a boring neighborhood recently abandoned for reasons I had no business finding out, or a cult-gnbor-hood that wants to sacrifice you for their demons.

Against anyone's better judgment, and after presumably being kidnapped with no one looking for me—making for a pretty free chance to escape—I explored the houses. Found nothing in the first five I came across, until I stumbled on one that still had snacks and some food, with a semi-futuristic microwave that still worked. Knowing I might not come across food for a while, I sat down, ate what I could, and saved the rest before heading back outside in search of more supplies.

Then somehow, I came across the basement—a weird section of the house that didn't have a door, just stairs leading down to your fated demise. I walked down, only seeing darkness as I struggled to find a light source—until I heard a click, and the room lit up with the dimmest of lights to guide me.

I saw nothing but a brown room with sinks, all neatly placed in order, without fail or even the slightest imperfection—leaving me awestruck with wonder at how such things could even exist. I left the basement empty-handed but gained a new respect for the world around me, furthering my motivation to get home and actually do something for this greater world.

After around two hours of aimlessly checking houses, I ended up finding a flashlight behind one of the last houses, with a weird battery of a brand I didn't recognize. Luckily, it was in English, reading:
"Quantum Battery – May your future hold the light to endless power."

With that, I headed back—walking in whatever direction I thought the road was. Hoping it wasn't too far, as I tend to be a lot slower when I'm full than even when I'm starving—plus the cramps. So with every bit of intent not to die at 15 before even getting a girlfriend (yes, I was a loner), I ran as fast as these bones and flesh could carry me—until I got tired in the endless grass fields that seemed to stretch on forever.

I lay down, exhausted, ready to just sleep until someone hopefully rescued me.

However—out of nowhere (and I have no idea if it was adrenaline or the sheer will not to die without leaving some mark on the world)—a sudden boost of energy kept me running until I finally found the road. And concurrently...
A car.

Part 2 of Section 1

Coming across this old—maybe early '80s to late '70s—car that, nowadays, fits this town all too well in this funny little planet of ever-advancing technology, always making things obsolete faster with ever-greater leaps. Anyways, the car was, oddly enough, unlocked with the key inside—conveniently within reach of my person.

Hopping into the car, it smelled like coffee beans—though I couldn't find any, so they must've already been taken out. Along with that, I found a charger, although I didn't know how to operate it—it was way too complex. It also just stuck out like a sore thumb compared to all the other low-tech junk in the car. Kinda makes you wonder where the person got it from... or even if it's theirs? The car might have even belonged to whoever the backpack belonged to, given its location.

I switched over to the driver's seat to see if the key was the right one—and sure enough, it was. Driving off down the gloomy roads with about 73 in the tank, which should've been enough to get at least out of state depending on where I was in the golden states. I tried to figure out how... well, not much happened next as everything went smoothly without any hiccups—until I ran low on gas.

Somehow, my luck streak was still going strong, because I came up on a gas station in a grassy area—this time, dark green grass —with a normal road behind a wall of green bushes or trees, all alone in the middle of nowhere.

As I got out of the car, I noticed some sparkly light from within the store that caught my eye. Investigating, I opened the door and got hit with a cold, fabric-like smell—only to see what can only be described as a fully metal suit sitting in the corner with a bullet wound in its head.

I checked it out, looking all over its slick body, realizing it wasn't a suit at all—it was some sort of robot I had never seen before in my life. Like one of those you see in movies or (more commonly) video games—completely human-looking but with a headpiece that's a screen. I also saw blood trailing from the counter. So whatever went down here... seems like the robot was attacking someone, and another person came from the back and popped a clean hole through it.

Hopefully, there aren't more around trying to attack me— especially with my only weapon not even having a clip!

Keeping this in mind, I hastily took the—
"Stack of credit cards? WHY ARE THERE JUST A RANDOM STACK OF CREDIT CARDS!!! WHO HOARDS A STACK OF CARDS IN A CONVENIENCE STORE!!!!!!!!!!!"

...Ahem. Excuse my sudden outburst. I was very panicked, as one can imagine—having been, again, presumably kidnapped by a cult and now seeing a robot that may have just tried to kill someone, with no idea if more are on my tail, tracking every trail

I make. For who is to say thy finest hour is not set in the gravest of stones…
I also make rhymes.

Getting back on track. After this, I presumably went into full-blown hysteria—putting the credit cards in the bag while laughing like a lunatic at my hopeless situation. Oh, the irony. Going back in, I just took whatever I could—every item I salvaged furthered my goal of survival. I tossed it all into the trunk of this old wagon of the west—once heralded as a champion of its time, now a relic.

I paced back and forth in a panic, constantly asking myself: "What am I going to do now?"

Knowing I would never get a truly satisfying answer.

I questioned if I should just give up as a rush of all my past mistakes filled my mind—until I cried. Laying there, past laid out like spilled ink, until I woke. I found a bottle of water, and with my dehydrated face, I said:
"Ay, who cares," and took a shot.

My worries went away on the spot. I felt energy—like I had just fueled up the car—so I got back
in and gladly drove off toward Phoenix, into the open, pitch-black abyss of what one would think
is night.

Surprisingly, this car is very fuel efficient. It took quite a while, but the fuel lasted decently long—until I started noticing I was getting back under again. Though at this point, I wasn't worried. With the fresh "water" still in my veins, I began to notice my vision blurring sometimes. But I was too distracted to even care about that—I just kept my hands on the steering wheel.

That was until I reached a crossroads when—
Oh, I can't even read the sign in front of me.

So what do you do in a predicament like this?
Turn into the intersection without bothering to get outside and just read it!
(It was for the best anyway, in the long run.)

Now I was truly just highballing, 'cause if I didn't know where I was, then I might as well guess. I might hit a board eventually.

So while driving, I check the speedometer—
and see I'm going 130.
Then—stop.

The car finally ran out of gas after driving at top speed for too long. I probably could've squeezed out another 2–3 hours if I wasn't being such a showoff.

To no one's surprise, I don't waste a second. I beeline it in a random direction I must have figured would be the best resting spot, as a hangover begins to set in with every step—through what is now a familiar wheat-grass plain of nothing. Somehow, I had returned to this dreaded area.

Maybe...
Maybe it was my fate—to die alone, sad, pride-less, with desperation being the last feeling I would ever feel—

When all of a sudden—
BONK

Section 2: Funny Meeting You Here of All Places

There is probably a 1 in how-many-squares/cities/states/whatever chance that this encounter could have taken place—if at all. Almost like there's some force out there letting these unbelievably low odds actually happen. Obviously.

This sudden contact of bodies resulted in me knocking someone flat onto the ground. Mind you—we are in an open field, with absolutely nothing blocking our view. I have no idea why she couldn't see me, but it's very clear why I couldn't see her. So in all fairness... it was her fault for not paying attention.

Still kinda dizzy, I don't immediately help her up, which only makes her more mad. She snaps, reminding me that she's still lying there, forcing me to help her instead of just standing up herself—one of her many personality traits.

I bend down, lend her a hand, and help her up. That's when I get a better look at her: black jacket with a hood covering her head, though I can still see the faint glow of her red hair. She's got a backpack too. And she's noticeably shorter than me. (*Why do I do this to myself?*)

With that, my first words to this complete stranger are:
"Hehe, short stack."

Clearly taken aback by this frankly adorable comment on her height and bodily shape, she yells at me:

"What did ye say, you bonny good-for-nothing! I 'ta beat you senseless for such foul mouthery!"
...with a mid-southern accent, no less.

I, still loopy and definitely in no shape to hold a proper conversation, slur back:

"Umm... not sure I understood that fully... Ya like being called a small wedding cake?"

And that sets off the tiny beast, as she goes on a rampage.

"If you dare say another word about my height, I swear to thou holiness I'ma beat ye so bad, they'll need a translexagronador to repair your broken bones!"

"Sounds fun. You okay with me laying down on you? I, myself, am feeling quite tired—and you look like a comfy pillow."

"No ye can not! In fact, ye can get ready for a beatdown!"

She lunges at me—swinging, missing, again and again. Her short arms just can't reach me as I dodge each attempt effortlessly. After a few minutes of this comedic back-and-forth, she begins to tire. Breathing heavily after every swing:

"Why are you so quick?! JUST STAND STILL ALREADY, YE TALL SKELETON!!"

I'm also pretty done with the constant dodging, so I try calming her down… in the worst way possible:

"You seem to be getting tired. You sure you can't spare a few hours for me to lay down on your thigh? I've been driving for, like, 1 or 2 days and I really need rest."

"Like I said—no—wait… you got a car?"

Suddenly, she freezes. Her ears perk up with interest like a goblin hearing rumors of nearby gold.
(Greedy bunch, goblins.)

"Yep. Though it's out of fuel, so unless you kn—"

"All ye need is some fuel, fellow? I just so happen to have come across some in the nearest town," she says, grinning deviously.

And my poor soul, none the wiser, believes every word this red-headed menace dares to speak.

"All ye gotta do is follow me, feller."

"Do you always call your boyfriends 'feller'?"

"No, that's what you call a stranger you want to be 'nice' to… feller."

And with that, we leave on our merry way…
to get some OIL.

Section 2, Part 2: Walking and Warnings

Walking never gets old in this backwards country. No matter how far we've come as a species, no matter how many advancements we make, we'll never overcome the primal urge to just walk this earth. After about 66 minutes of silent trudging, I completely pass out—sleepwalking without realizing it.

That's when the stranger kindly wakes me up with a voice like an angel.

"Wake up, Bonesington. We're almost at the place. You can see it up ahead."

"O... oooh. Who are you? Wait—what happened to the... THE CAR RAN OUT OF GAS!! OoooOOoooh, this day cannot get any worse. Now how the hell am I supposed to get back to Phoenix?!"

I shout, the last of the "fresh water" finally worn off.

"Calm down, feller. I know ye don't know me, but if it makes ya feel any better, my name's Jelly.

Jelly Hockings. Kinda a famous name around these parts."

"Unless you're the president, a government official, or someone who can get me out of here—I don't care."

I stop walking, wanting answers.

"Look—you want the 'gas' or not? 'Cause if not, I'm just gonna take your car."

I notice the shotgun strapped behind her back—the kind that does real damage. Fatal damage.

"Y-Yeah, cool. So... where are we heading, Jell?"

"Jelly!"

"Got you, got you..."

I grumble, already knowing what would happen if I keep mispronouncing her name.

We keep walking as she lays out a very motivating plan—motivating in the "do this or die" kind of way.

"Here's what you and me are gonna do. Oh—and what's your name, feller?"

"Tom. Tom Batchelor. Mi-Grayer."

"...So just Tom?"

"Yeah."

"Okay. You and I will go in together. If you hear any sleek mechanical sounds, I suggest praying to whatever god you believe in—and running for the hills."

"Metaphorically or—?"

"No. The southern hills. Just north of here. Pretty much the only way you're escaping them."

"Escape what? Wait... are you saying those robot things were at the gas station?!"

"Maybe. What number did it have next to it, Tom?"

"01."

"Then yeah. Once we get in—if we don't die—you lead me to your car immediately. The longer we stay inside, the greater the risk of those bots taking us straight to the slaughterhouse."

"Sure. Whatever doesn't get me killed."

With the "plan" set, we enter the town with nothing to our names but some vague optimism and a little too much caffeine-like adrenaline.

It doesn't take long before Jelly spots a suspiciously futuristic office building—some odd, complex structure that stands out even in this messed-up place. She stops at the entrance and says:

"Try not to die."

A harder task than it sounds, in hindsight. I wish every day that I could change what came next.

We enter the facility completely silent. From here on, it's total stealth—just in case there's a robot lurking around. Jelly starts using hand signals to direct me. Sometimes they make sense. Most of the time, they don't. Still, it somehow helps.

The rooms are like a massive power plant fused with a sci-fi tech lab. Unfortunately, whatever the scientists were working on here had already been moved, looted, or obliterated.

We manage to bag four quantum batteries—the square kind that Jelly says are way more powerful than the ones I found before. We find them in what's probably the main server room. There's also a lone laptop just sitting there. Of course, it needs a password.

So, we move deeper—finding a jump starter, the kind that connects to the quantum batteries to directly inject energy into whatever you need. Like a car jumper, but on steroids. We grab that too.

Further down, we stumble on old assembly lines—stuff that was probably used for mass production. At one point, we spot a barrel, but Jelly warns it might be a trap. Apparently, the bots use decoys to lure people into dark, hard-to-escape places.

So we leave it alone.

Eventually, we reach what looks like the control room. Empty, stripped down—but the security cameras are still up. Sort of. They're bizarre-looking, but they're not functional. Just static.

Oddly enough, we do find something valuable: the password for the laptop, and a device labeled USP—a "Universal Save File Pro." Basically an upgraded USB.

"Why change the 'B' to a 'P'?"

"No idea. Sounds cooler, I guess."

While I'm examining it, we get that distinct "you're being watched" feeling. Something—or someone—is stalking us. Waiting.

We're about to head to the next floor when we see... it. Another bot. Sticker 01. Standing right in front of us, ready to strike.

We don't stick around.

We bolt.
Except—like an absolute psychopath—Jelly turns around, pulls her shotgun, and—"WHAT ARE YOU DOING?! ARE YOU CRA—"

I don't even finish before she 360s the damn thing—spinning twice and blasting a clean hole right through its metal skull. She flies back into a wall from the recoil.

I rush to her, help her up, and mumble a compliment.

"Damn. That was... impressive."

She blushes slightly—her pride swelling with praise she definitely doesn't deserve.

(Ahem. I mean, she doesn't not deserve.)

After the chaos, we both agree: nope. We are not checking the bot's body. Instead, we head to the second floor.

There, we find a white room labeled "Experimental Lab." Inside, there's a glowing device labeled *Cellunate*. No clue what it does.

Next room: two suits. One is a sleek black combat outfit. The other, a movie-style hazmat suit. Naturally, we take both. I also snag a cool mask and toss it into my backpack.

We change in separate rooms. I just slip the suit under my clothes (and sneak in a shower—my first since I got here). Jelly puts hers over her outfit.

As the wise man said: "Better to be safe than."

We head into the next room and—surprise!—there it is. The gas can.

Turns out, we didn't need the suits at all.

We also find a weapon: an AR-15SK—a modified version of the classic rifle. Naturally, I take it.

With our loot secured—Jelly carrying the gas can, me holding the laptop—we head out... until we're ambushed.

A faster version of the last robot nearly takes my head off. But somehow, my body reacts on pure reflex demon mode, dodging without thinking.

It makes a beeline for Jelly—but before she can shoot, another bot attacks from behind and knocks her shotgun away.

Despite never firing a gun before, the suit—and maybe my 10,000 hours of Call of Duty—kick in. I pull the trigger and doink both in the head. Headshots. Every time.

More bots close in. Jelly grabs her shotgun while I cover her, landing shot after shot—Ultra Instinct style. We're surrounded, but hold our ground.

Until—

A loud sound echoes through the building.

The bots... back off.

One by one.

We take the moment to celebrate. Jelly even offers something close to gratitude.

"Nice save back there. I really owe you one."

"Any time, missy. Any time."

Right before—

Another scream sends us running. Full sprint. Back to the ladder. Back out of this hellhole.

Once outside, we see what caused the sound:

A massive robot-beast hybrid. More monster than machine. Hard to make out, but... horrifying.

I remember the mask. Curious if it could block out the sound, I foolishly decide to try it on.

"Hey, Jelly—what is this mask, anyway?"

She asks again and again, but her voice seems far away. I'm drawn to it—like a moth to a flame.

Or a snap from a hypnotist.

The moment I put it on—

Shock. From every nerve.

Every direction.

And then—

Darkness.

Part 3 - Section 2

The air outside feels colder now than it ever has. You can feel the breeze like a summer wind cutting through mid-spring's chill — a feeling I hadn't experienced in a long time. There's a tension in the air, like a string pulled too tight, ready to snap. Jelly and I walk the cold stone path that fate, in all its unfairness, has laid out for us. Still, I dare not question its choices — what use is arguing with gods over what is and what isn't? That's a surefire way to draw more wrath than answers.

The fallen one warned me:

"You never stood a chance out there. Best play by their rules — no matter how cruel the consequences for disobedience. Or do you wish to end up as I did? I'm not called the Fallen Angel for nothing."

But I don't fear death — not anymore. The fallen one and I...

we have plans. Bigger than either of us. But I ask myself —
truly ask: Do I want to stay dead? To never know what I'm
capable of? Or will I rise — live — and fight for something
greater?

T̃OM̲ : "—— ERROR FOUND IN CODE ——"
anxiety/CLASS: NEGATIVE FOUND
SYSTEM REBOOT IN: 10… 9… 8…

"TOM!… You still breathing?"

"It's time to wake up, ToM…"

I gasped awake, breathing heavy for what felt like minutes
before realizing the mask I had put on… was lying on the
ground. I picked it up, stupidly, and shoved it back in my
backpack — probably a mistake — and sat there, panicking. Jell
crouched beside me, trying to calm me down.

Once I finally got a hold of myself, I said,

"Why does it feel like I got hit by Zeus? Was I out long?"

"Only two hours. I was planning on leaving, but figured I should
wait — it's almost night."

"Wait… like without me?"

"Who's to say."

I paused, then:
"…Do I have a British accent or did I hit my head too hard on
the gravel, mate?"

"Nope, it's 100% there. You ain't going crazy — yet."

Then something clicked in my head.
"Say… you wouldn't happen to be related to a Miss Jennifer Hockings, would you?"

She smiled.
"Of course I am — she was my grandma. Hard to believe a young Texan gal like me comes from that kind of legacy, huh?"

"Wait—your grandmother? That can't be right. I knew her… we were classmates. Last I checked, she didn't have any kin."

"You mean my mother, right? People didn't really talk about her much in the media — publicity reasons. But what shocks me is you not knowing who she is. You sure you're from around here?"

"No, no… we were classmates…" I trailed off. "Wait. What year is it?"

"2145."

My heart stopped.
"No. No, that's not possible. It was 2026…"

"119 years ago," she replied matter-of-factly.
"Exactly 200 years since World War II ended, actually. Funny, huh?"

I just stared at the road ahead. Everything hit me at once — the tech, the robots, the factory, the *quantum batteries*. It all made sense now.

"That explains the futuristic tech," I muttered.

Jell nodded, playing along — whether from pity or genuine confusion, I couldn't tell.
"Probably. After the Great Solar Flare wiped out 99% of Earth's electricity for 10 years, only quantum fuel and high-powered atomic energy could run anything. This village was likely near a production zone for that tech — explains the factory. Places like that gave out quantum tools cheaper than the originals for locals."

I didn't respond. I couldn't. I was emotionally wrecked — 134 years old on paper. Everyone I ever knew was likely dead, my name forgotten. Including the person sitting right next to me — a descendant of someone I once knew better than most.

Once we reached the car, we quietly packed everything in the trunk. Jell refueled it, and we climbed in.

"Did she ever… mention me?" I whispered.

"Hmm? You say something, partner?"

"Oh, um… where are you headed?"

She turned the key and grinned.
"The Grid. So I can save the world and live up to expectations set long before I was born."

I slouched in my seat, trying not to break.
"Then I guess that makes two of us."

"So… you also want to be a hero? Because you don't look very battle-ready, no offense."

"No. I've got nothing left. No past. No future. So why not go with the one thing that still knows my name?"

She glanced at me, more serious now.
"You're really not pretending, are you?"

"I wish I was."

She smirked.
"Off to Oklahoma… then the Kansas State Grid!"

Section 3 – The Finale: Will This Endless Loop Just End?

The road — an endless streamlined feature, once built to improve travel for vehicles (cars, trucks, SUVs, A.M.s) — now stretches before us like a monument to a dead dream. It once made the country feel more connected, a lavish dream realized in less than 50 years after the invention of the automobile. But now, it's a bitter, hollow thing — a symbol of what once brought people together but now has no one left to carry.

A terrible irony.
I wrote something like that during a pit stop to cool off the radiator. I'm pretty sure the entry is still saved on that old terminal we found. The storm was brewing ahead — thick, foggy clouds rolling like ghosts across the Texas horizon, or what I've confirmed is Texas through the IPSG: International Ping Servers for Global use — GPS 2.0. Its maps are rendered in such high detail, I almost began to question if they were more real than the dead road right in front of us.

Unfortunately, I can't access any of the apps — they're encrypted behind passwords or security keys I don't have. Bored, I tried browsing the web for entertainment, only to find nothing. None of the old websites I knew exist anymore. Hell, even the search engines themselves are extinct.

Now I rely on my senior-by-two-years granddaughter for basic web searches. So this is what it means to be old, I thought. Every waking day I grow older in a world where I should've long been dead. Some would call this a gift — the chance to live in a future their timeline never promised them. But not me. I just want my old, mediocre life back, even if it meant dying yesterday, again.

What good is a second chance if you can't even figure out how to survive in a world that treats your memories like myths?

But enough of that. The radiator cooled, and we were ready to roll again. We crossed the Oklahoma state border in just under four minutes — nearly to the safe zone. We weren't in any rush, thankfully — we had three days' worth of extra fuel.

That's when I got called grandpa.

It was some prepubescent jab from Jell after I made a comment about how things used to be less complicated.

"Yeah? And how old are you — twenty?"
She grinned. "Sixteen."
"I'm fifteen! And you're calling me gramps?"

She smirked like she'd just won a prize.
"You mean 134? Not exactly springing with youth at that age."

That started another one of our usual arguments:
Am I old because I was born over a century ago?
Or am I young because I've only lived fifteen of those years?

We never reach a conclusion. We just switch topics. This time,
she points at my drink.

"Is that alcohol?"
"No. It's fresh 'water.' Says so on the label."
"Definitely alcohol. Explains why you tried to hit on me when
we first met. FYI, putting quotes around it is a dead giveaway
— people do that to hide booze."

I ignored the flirting comment and focused on the drink.
"Why would they go through the trouble of labeling it like
that?"

"The Act of 86 banned alcohol outright. In the 2080s, booze
accounted for about 34% of the U.S. death rate. So they nuked it
from the Union. No one really respects the law now, but they
still put 'fresh water' on it as a subtle middle finger."

"Cool. Wait, what did you say about me hitting on you?"

"Nothing."
She shot me that look — the one older sisters give their younger
brothers when they want them to
shut up.

(And I should know. I had one.)

Section 3, Part 3 – "Unexpected Company"

With that, we traveled the rest of the way through the border states. We were entering Oklahoma under a stormy overcast sky. Despite the looming clouds, the rain never came — the storm passed in under an hour. Accounting for the time zone shift, we estimated we'd arrive in just about an hour, so long as nothing distracted us.

Of course, that's exactly when Jell spotted something on the roadside.

At first, it looked like a robot. She insisted it was something different. I pleaded with her to ignore it — but predictably, she turned the car around.

We pulled up to the area she pointed to. Sure enough, it was there: a fully intact robot, oddly pristine compared to the scorched surroundings. Tiny rocks scattered around what could've been mistaken for a blast crater. The thing sat slumped against a metal pole, powered down.

Before I could stop her, Jell jumped out and rushed toward it — confusing the American out of me.

"Jell! Maybe it's not the best idea to get close to one of those machines! What if it's playing dead?"
"I knew it had to be a different model. Could it be a prototype?"
"Tom, get over here. You need to see this!"

Grudgingly, I followed. The first thing I noticed was the

number *0.9* stamped on its side — different from the 01 we'd seen on the last one.

"What do you think the 0.9 means?"
"Could be a prototype, or maybe they started using decimals after version 03."
(*Did she say 03…?*)
"Wait — there are more of these things?"
"Yeah. We've only found 01 and 03 so far. There've been sightings of 02, but if they're true, that makes at least three versions."
"Three?! We barely survived the first one, and now you're telling me there's levels to this?!"
"And maybe even more — if you really want to get into conspiracy theories."
"What's the difference between them? Are we fighting demons? Monsters? Runners? Boosters?
Gods? Because I'm not sure I can take this anymore!"

"Hold your horses. I'll explain once we're back in the car. But first — I want to see if I can bring this one with us for research. This is going to be sick."

"Wait — don't! Don't touch i—"

Too late. The moment she touched the robot's metallic side, a powerful shockwave erupted. It knocked us both off our feet. The robot stirred — and then stood up.

I swear, my soul nearly left my body.
We stood there frozen, suddenly aware we'd both left our guns in the car like a pair of idiots. Panic surged. On instinct, I

"Partner… you're crushing me."
"Sorry! Sorry…" I muttered, backing off awkwardly.

Then the robot spoke — in a cold, mechanical tone:

"Partner: when two humans are in what is defined as a romantic relationship that is doomed to fail."
"OKAY. That was rude, you scrap-yard metal phony!"
"Jell… it just spoke! And you're mad about its comment on our relationship?"
"Robots talk all the time where I'm from, Mr. Fossil. And partner meant business partner, thank you very much."
"Understood, Ms. Jellition and Mr. Fossil. According to my data log, this unit is named Survivor, so I will assume that as my name."

Still insulted, Jell scoffed.
"Tom, we should just leave him here. He's messing with us on purpose — and it's annoying."
"Hmm… I'm on board with that. Let me just get the car—"

The robot interrupted.
"You are leaving in a vehicle. May I accompany you? I would like to leave this hot area."

"Only if you call us by our real names."
(You don't even do that, I mumbled.)
"Yes, Jell and Tom."
"Close enough," Jell said. "But it's Jelly. I'll let you off the hook. You can join our little operation."
"OK, Miss Jelly."

And with that, we packed up. The robot climbed into the car, and we sped off toward Oklahoma City — with more questions than answers, and one strange new passenger.

Section 3 Finale – "I'M SAVED!!!"

When you're driving, it's good manners to make sure your passengers are comfortable. However, there are exceptions — like when doing so risks the driver's sanity. Case in point: this damn robot.

The thing spent the rest of the trip interrupting every single conversation Jell and I tried to have. If not for her insisting it'd be "worth it in the end," I would've kicked that metal loudmouth out of the car at 70 miles per hour.

It should have been worth it.

But instead, it just jabbered until we somehow started reminiscing about how we met.
"So pretty much, we bumped into each other — got me a bit mad — but I kept my cool. Until you stood up and started flirting with me, which made me even more mad—"

Jell couldn't hold back her laughter and burst into hysterical giggles, like a coyote on moonshine, which only made my face heat up more.

"Okay, okay, I wasn't at my best! It was just a little mistake."
"Tell that to me after you fell asleep while walking. Snort."
"Pig."

"And I'm guessing after that, I woke up to you threatening to shoot me because you couldn't find
the car?"
"Well, I am a wild gal — that's what my friends and family always say."
"Totally. 'That's what my friends say about me.' Yeah, sure."

Then I remembered something.

"Speaking of — your last name is Hocking, right?"
"Mhm. Our family's got a long-standing scientific legacy. My great-great-grandpapi was Stephen Hocking."
"…The guy who was on the Epstein list?"

"What list?"

That's when the robot chimed in — because of course it did.

"Epstein's Island. A remote location most commonly known for housing rich pre—"
"*Shush*, you robot dictionary!"
"Yes, sire."

"What about the island? My great-great-grandpapi was listed on it?"
"Oh, nothing. Just... a pre-show trivia thing."
"Okay, I'll believe ye. But if I find out you were badmouthing him, you're dead meat."

Before I could grill it further, Jell pointed ahead.

"Hey, look — it's the gates to the city."

We were finally there. The gates to Oklahoma City, District 92 Outpost.

And with that realization, the weight of everything we'd been through hit me like a brick wall wrapped in joy.

I shouted out with everything I had:

"I'M SAVED!!!"

And that's all I've got for this round of the recap.
Join me next time on HPG CAST!
See ya next time, fold.

...part 4.

Evelyn Washburn

Evelyn Washburn is a student at WISH Academy High School who enjoys exploring realistic, emotional themes in literature. Writing has always been a passion of hers, and as a young girl in elementary school, she dreamed of becoming an author one day. Although her favorite genre has shifted over time, going from fantasy to realistic fiction to poetry, writing has always been an outlet for her to express herself and share the stories of characters she's created in her mind. When she's not writing, she can be found at her dance studio or reading a book quietly in the corner. This is her third published story, and likely not her last!

Bring Me to the Surface
by Evelyn Washburn

I miss the time when each day was carefree.
The only thing that mattered was to have fun.
We were so young and naive,
And unaware of what's to come.
As our elementary years passed by,
We spared no time to appreciate the memories slipping through
our fingers like water.

Soon enough,
We'll find that sunny days are no longer bright,
That rainy days are no longer rare,
And that storms are festering in our subconscious.

As we approach adulthood, we start to learn.
We learn about the true nature of life,
The true nature of humans,
The true nature of people we thought we knew.
We are no selfless species.

In our adolescence, we start to take on more responsibility.
School becomes harder,
Relationships begin to change,
And we start to get lost in the waves.

We fight and fight to get that fun high school experience,
But each new day is met with another pile of work;
Another downpour atop our heads.
We strive to keep our grades up while maintaining friendships,
We struggle to keep our families happy and healthy,
Yet the tide is slowly coming in,
Creeping up behind us unnoticed.

While everyone works hard,
There are only so many spots available in every position.
You may not be as qualified, experienced, or confident as
someone else,
And so many fail to get the ideal life of their dreams.
Every day is a competition,

And while we can't call it that directly,
It's always haunting us from the shadows.
In this modern world, everyone must give one hundred percent
and beyond,
Because otherwise, we'll get lost and fall behind.

Nothing comes without hard work.
Our younger selves were oblivious to this fact,
But now, much to our dismay, we have learned to accept it,
For even those born with a silver spoon become aware,
As it hits us like a sudden tsunami of responsibility.

Learning to be independent paves a new path for you.
A path where no one walks beside you.
It teaches you how to fend for yourself.
It teaches you that the only one you can truly trust,
Is yourself.
So while you drown in waves of work,
You become too afraid to reach out.

In the middle of the ocean, I am stranded.
There is not a single soul nearby.
I am left here,
Cold and alone, being tossed left and right, up and down by the
waves.

"You're not good enough."

Life stood still,
But now life is a whirlwind of emotions,
Of thoughts,
Of work,
So much work.

And while I'm busy trying to be my best self,
I'm sinking.
I'm plummeting into the deep depths of the water.
My lungs are slowly filling up.
I can't scream for help,
But who would I scream for?

I wasted time investing myself in work,
I neglected my friendships to be as perfect as I could be,
I was constantly worrying about only myself.
How selfish.

And now the weight of it all comes crashing down.
The tides have turned against me.
I'm at the breaking point.
My lungs are filled to the brim.
I can't breathe, can't think, can't speak, can't see,
Can't work.
I'm completely, utterly useless in this state of oblivion.

But a light starts to shine.
Breaking through the tension on the surface of the water is a
hand.
I muster all my strength to grab that hand,
And that hand grabs hold of me while I grip with everything I
have left.

I come crashing out of the whirlwind.
My thoughts slow.
My heart races.
My senses are overloaded, but I feel something I haven't felt for
years.
Hope.

Sometimes, all you need is for that one person to be there for you.
The one person who listens when you think you're just complaining.
The one person who will do anything to protect your well-being.
The one person who understands you.
The one person who will bring you to the surface.

That is what truly appreciating life is.
No one can be perfect,
And striving for perfection only leaves you in shambles.
Building a lifelong relationship to lean on is what keeps you afloat in the ocean.

Think back to the years of your childhood,
The years where you weren't worried about the future and expectations.
Those were the golden years of your life,

And now it's time for you to accept,
That while life is hard,
You are the only one who can give yourself happiness.
You are the only one who fully understands how you feel.
You are the only one who can choose to truthfully confide in a friend.

Regardless of what your mind might say,
There are people out there to support you.
So don't stay dormant,
Don't stay alone.
Go out there into the world,
And find someone to bring you to the surface.

Acknowledgments

We want to thank Sammie, Z. Zar Zar, Jerron, Jason, Xander, Kiani, Veronica, Philip, Analise, Etienne, Luc, Bowie, Judah, Tristan, Kristy, Ryan, Adrienne, Abby, Adetoni, Autumn, Daniil, Qi'yanna, Jessica, Kai, Mariah, Treyce, Grace, Theori, & Evelyn for sharing their stories, poems, and art with the world.

May your words inspire others as you have inspired us! With courage, honesty, and creativity, you remind us of the power within every young heart.

This book is for you—your dreams, your journeys, and the bright futures you are shaping.

We would also like to thank all the parents, caregivers, and adults who have supported their students and encouraged them to use their voices to speak their minds.

Finally, a big thank you to Cynthia Avalos for supporting the idea of a student anthology. Thank you for inspiring your students and agreeing to let us publish their words. We couldn't have done this without you.